The elevator doors opened, and he was dumped onto the fourth floor.

Rounding the corner, he frowned when he spied Rachel in one of the chairs. Hell, he hoped this wasn't about what had happened between them last year. In all honesty, he'd been waiting for that to catch up with him.

You're being paranoid, Seb.

They'd both been consenting adults who'd agreed to remain mum about the night they'd shared. Not that the hospital really had any rules against colleagues sleeping together, although the unspoken consensus was that it could be a sticky situation. But it evidently worked for some. There was at least one pair of surgeons at Centre Hospitalier who were married. He and Rachel weren't even close to being married or involved, though. It had been just one night.

Rachel didn't even look at him. Dressed in a gauzy white skirt and a blouse that was as blue as the ocean, she looked almost as warm and inviting. And when she crossed her legs in that slow slide of calf over her swallowed.

Okay, a

Dear Reader,

As a parent, I have had my share of scary moments. Our family has been through a couple of sets of stitches, a broken bone and a whole slew of minor ailments. But the worst was when my daughter started having persistent pain in her thigh, and we were sent to an orthopedist. He ordered X-rays to look for anomalies in her femur. What went unspoken in the room that day was one of my greatest fears: cancer. Fortunately, it turns out that her joints were just too flexible and that was causing her pain.

But what if it *had* been cancer? That moment in my daughter's life provided the inspiration for Sebastien and Rachel's story. Because not everyone leaves their doctor's office with sighs of relief. These two characters touched my heart in a way that made them linger long after the last line of the book was written. I'm so glad you've chosen to journey to a gorgeous island in French Polynesia to meet Seb and Rachel! I hope that as they battle their way through the past and try to banish lurking fears, you too are touched. Thank you for reading their story.

Love,

Tina Beckett

A FAMILY MADE
IN PARADISE

———

TINA BECKETT

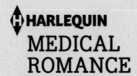

HARLEQUIN
MEDICAL
ROMANCE

Recycling programs for this product may not exist in your area.

ISBN-13: 978-1-335-73738-0

A Family Made in Paradise

Copyright © 2022 by Tina Beckett

For questions and comments about the quality of this book, please contact us at CustomerService@Harlequin.com.

Harlequin Enterprises ULC
22 Adelaide St. West, 41st Floor
Toronto, Ontario M5H 4E3, Canada
www.Harlequin.com

Printed in U.S.A.

Three-time Golden Heart® finalist **Tina Beckett** learned to pack her suitcases almost before she learned to read. Born to a military family, she has lived in the United States, Puerto Rico, Portugal and Brazil. In addition to traveling, Tina loves to spend time with her family, hit the trails on her horse and cuddle with her pug, Alex. Learn more about Tina from her website, or "friend" her on Facebook.

Books by Tina Beckett

Harlequin Medical Romance

The Island Clinic collection

How to Win the Surgeon's Heart

New York Bachelor's Club

Consequences of Their New York Night
The Trouble with the Tempting Doc

A Summer in São Paulo

One Hot Night with Dr. Cardoza

Risking It All for the Children's Doc
It Started with a Winter Kiss
Starting Over with the Single Dad
Their Reunion to Remember
One Night with the Sicilian Surgeon
From Wedding Guest to Bride?

Visit the Author Profile page
at Harlequin.com for more titles.

To my children.

CHAPTER ONE

Centre Hospitalier de Taurati was no place for children. Especially not this time of year. Not any time of year, really, but especially not when school was out. Sebastien Deslaurier turned the corner to head to a patient's room and almost collided with someone. He swerved, turning his head to mutter an apology, only to tense when he recognized who it was.

Damn.

They both stopped and eyed each other in the same way they had for the last year. With a wariness that said they'd rather be anywhere but face-to-face. Or body to body.

She spoke first. "Sorry." Her voice had an odd tremble.

It wasn't her fault. He hadn't been paying attention, either. But he was now. "What's wrong?"

Her chin went up. "Who said anything was wrong?"

But there was. He'd sat with enough worried parents to know the fear that threaded through mundane phrases.

"Rachel…" His tongue traitorously savored those two syllables, hanging on to them for an instant before releasing them into the air. He swallowed, trying not to remember other times he'd said her name. On a night that had been as hot as their single fiery encounter.

She gave a half shrug, as if she hadn't noticed his struggle. "It's nothing. My daughter is a bit under the weather this morning, that's all. I'm having her seen."

That brought him back to earth with a bump. He knew all about Rachel Palmer's daughter. It was one of the reasons he tended to steer clear of her. His son had died. While her daughter had lived.

Dammit, not something either of them could help. And it wasn't fair for him to judge her based on that. Hell, his infant son's cancer diagnosis was the whole reason he'd gone into pediatrics years ago.

Speaking of which…why was Rachel standing in front of the exam room door he was about to go in? He glanced down at the patient he'd been called to look at and swallowed. Claire *Palmer*. How could he not have put two and two together?

"Claire is who I'm here to examine, actually."

"You?" Her eyes widened, and she edged closer to the door. "I thought Dr. Rogan was the on-call pediatrician today. If I'd known, I'd have…"

Her voice trailed away.

She would have what? Refused to let him see her? Taken her daughter to another medical facility? He hadn't thought they'd left things on such bad terms that night a year ago. But maybe he was wrong.

And Claire?

How did you ask someone whose child had had cancer if she was afraid it had returned? You didn't. You simply offered an ear. "Why don't you tell me what's going on with her?"

She shook her head. "I would have taken her to an urgent care center. I probably should have, actually. But I figured they would just send me back here." She bit her lip. "I'm hoping I'm being ridiculous and that you'll tell me it's just a virus."

Just a virus. But it wasn't said with a chirp of self-deprecating laughter. Instead there was strange sense of desperation. It was there in her eyes. The way her fingers twisted together again and again. As if she were pleading with the universe to not let it be what she feared it was.

He remembered exactly how that felt.

If that was it, why had she almost taken her daughter to urgent care rather than bringing her here to the hospital? Was she afraid he'd wind up being the attending if she had?

Actually, her comment about thinking that Dr. Rogan was the on-call physician seemed to bear that out.

He could understand why, if so. Their periodic interactions were nothing if not awkward, despite their assurances that their one wild night together meant nothing.

It evidently meant enough to make them steer clear of each other as much as possible.

"Dr. Rogan is taking care of an emergency case, so he asked me to see his next patient." He glanced at the door behind her. "Who is behind that door, I assume."

Rachel nodded. "I just stepped out for a second to give her some privacy while she changed into a hospital gown."

"In that case, why don't you give me a quick rundown on her symptoms before I go in?"

"Fever, lack of appetite, nausea…" There was a long pause. "And a swollen lymph node on the right side of her neck."

And there it was. The real reason why she was so scared.

"This is a new symptom?"

She nodded. "She hasn't had one of those since her…"

Since her cancer diagnosis.

The thought came through loud and clear. His brain worked through some alternatives.

He had to fight back his own sense of déjà vu. "COVID test?"

"That was my first thought. We did a rapid test, and it came back negative."

Of course she had. Rachel was a smart woman. She would rule out what she could on her own before asking for help.

"Let's go in, and I'll examine her."

He gave a quick knock on the door. A voice that was much more cheerful than her mother's said, "Come in."

Letting Rachel enter the room ahead of him, he saw that Claire was already sitting on the exam table. Rachel went to her daughter's side, while Sebastien took the opportunity to study the girl as he casually made his way over. He could see the swollen spot on the right side of her jaw even from this distance. If he remembered right, she'd had Hodgkin's lymphoma. Swollen lymphs were a classic sign of the condition.

"Hi, Claire, I'm Sebastien Deslaurier. You can call me Seb, if that's okay with your mom."

He glanced at her, catching her frown, but she gave a jerky nod of permission.

Continuing, he pulled up a stool and sat next to the bed. "Why don't you tell me what's going on? Starting with your symptoms. What did you notice first?"

"You mean this time? Or since I was born?" Her grin caught Seb by surprise. He couldn't stop the smile that formed on his own face.

"You remember your birth?"

"Well, no. Mom would have to tell you about that. I'm sure it was traumatic."

"Claire!" Rachel's quick admonition came from behind him.

He glanced back at her, the smile still on his face. "Don't worry, we don't need to go back that far." He turned his attention back to Claire. "Just since you started feeling sick this time."

Claire was a carbon copy of her mom, with dark brown hair and eyes that sparkled. Damn. There was so much zest for life here. He hoped to hell it wasn't what Rachel feared. The last thing he wanted was to have to break the news to her that her daughter's cancer was back.

"I got a sore throat a couple of nights ago. I didn't say anything, because I spent the night with friends a week ago and thought I caught something. But then no one else felt sick. Then last night, I felt sick and threw up. And I have this knot." She fingered the spot on her neck. She looked at him with an expression that said it all. "I know that worries my mom the most."

A ball of emotion lodged itself in his gut, and a million memories came skittering along his nerve endings.

So that he wouldn't focus on that, he picked up the electronic chart and glanced at it. "We'll get it sorted out." He glanced at Rachel. "They've already taken vitals?"

"Yes."

He perused what was recorded. Slightly elevated heart rate and blood pressure. And her temperature was still at 101. Low-grade fever. Another sign. "Do we have her records from the States?"

"I can get them transferred. But—"

"Let's start with that." He glanced at Claire. "I want to examine you and then get some blood drawn, okay?"

She shrugged. "I'm not scared of needles. I've seen plenty of them. And my mom's a nurse, so she's talked me through a lot of things."

Like PICC lines and MRIs?

"I'm sure she has." He smiled at the girl, hoping it looked more genuine than it felt.

The idea of being a doctor hadn't even been on his horizon when his boy had been diagnosed. But afterward? Hell, yes.

He made a call to the nurses' station about the blood draw.

Then he examined Claire, listening to her heart and lungs and having her lie back on the table so he could palpate her stomach. Nothing out of the ordinary.

He helped her sit back up. "I'm going to feel your neck. Tell me if anything hurts."

Placing his fingertips just below her ears, he walked them down, feeling for any abnormalities. The node on her right side wasn't huge, but it was large enough to be seen if you knew what you were looking for. He watched if she flinched when he pressed it, but she just sat stoically. "Hurt?"

"No, not really."

Hell, he'd been hoping the thing hurt like crazy. Enlarged nodes from Hodgkin's were rarely painful.

He continued down, checking her thyroid for nodules, but there was nothing. Other than the lymph node. "How's your throat?"

"It's okay. It was sore when I woke up, but…" She glanced at her mom before quickly adding, "It's better now."

Was she minimizing symptoms because she

knew how worried her mom was? He checked her throat, but her tonsils looked clear, and there was no sign of strep. But he'd take a throat swab anyway, just in case.

One of the pediatric nurses came in just as he was finishing up. She smiled at Rachel. "I know you're worried, Mom, but I'm sure she'll be fine. Especially with Dr. Sebastien on the case."

How could she be sure, when Sebastien wasn't? Him having anything to do with whether or not Claire would be fine wasn't really up to him.

He moved over to where Rachel was standing as the woman drew the prescribed number of vials. "I'm going to have a spot test for mono done as well. It takes about an hour."

"Yes, I know. I thought of that as well, but I haven't heard of any cases at her school or among her friends. Have there been any here at Hospitalier?"

There hadn't been. "Not that I know of, but that doesn't rule that or the flu out. I want to do a second COVID test as well, just for peace of mind."

"Thank you for being willing to see her."

Did she really think he was that much of a cad? That he'd realize who Claire was and then turn around and walk away because of their night together? He hoped she thought more of his professionalism than that. "Of course. Is Dr. Rogan her normal pediatrician?"

"Yes. But we've only seen him once, to get her health certificate before enrolling her in school. She's been so healthy, we haven't needed to see him…until now." Her voice had dropped almost to a whisper.

The nurse finished up and exited the room.

Claire turned to them. "See? No tears."

"I never doubted you for a minute." The girl's demeanor was engaging and every bit as winsome as her greeting had been. He felt a tug of something akin to affection in his gut.

Hell, he was glad Dr. Rogan was her primary care physician. He'd been involved with her mother. The last thing he needed was to have Claire as one of his patients.

As if reading his thoughts, Rachel went over and kissed her daughter on her head. "I'm going to step outside with Dr. Deslaurier. I'll be back in in a minute."

"Okay." Claire looked at him. "I'm sure I'll see you around, since my mom works here."

He forced yet another smile, his stomach churning. He hoped not. Hoped there'd be no need for the girl to make regular trips to Hospitalier. "I'm sure you will."

He and Rachel went into the hallway. He

headed off anything she might have been about
to say. "I'll let you know when I get the test results back. Until then, try not to worry."

"Easy for you to say."

No, it wasn't. But there was no way he was
going to tell her anything about his son. Not
only because it would make an already awkward situation between them even more awkward, but because he didn't talk about Bleu
to anyone. He dragged his hand through his
hair.

"Listen, I know this isn't easy. And not just
because of what happened…before." If he was
trying to make her feel better, he was botching
things. Time to retreat while he could. "I want
you to know, if you need me—for anything—
all you have to do is ask."

And that did *not* come out the way he'd expected it to, either. He quickly inserted, "For a
second look, I mean."

There was silence for few seconds before one
side of her mouth quirked. "Of course. What
else could you possibly have meant?"

Oh, she knew exactly the thought that had
crossed his mind as soon as the words were
out of his mouth. Had it crossed hers as well?

He wasn't going to stand around, though,
and let his memories drift back into forbidden
places. And if he kept talking, that's exactly

what was bound to happen. But he couldn't quite let her challenge go without a fitting response. He lowered his voice, allowing himself to taste her name one last time. "I think we both know the answer to that… Rachel."

Big mistake. He shouldn't have referred to her by her first name, because the cells at the very center of his brain—where dormant things were sent for storage—woke up. And they woke up with a vengeance.

Her fingers went up to smooth a lock of silky black hair as she reacted to his words, and her tongue flicked out to moisten her lips, making those newly awakened brain cells dance with kinetic energy.

Then she blinked, her hand dropping back to her side. "Well, I need to get back to her."

"And I need to get going, too, and see if Dr. Rogan has any more patients for me." Not that she needed to know anything about that. The need to end their conversation on a more serious note forced its way through him. "I hope the tests all come back clean. I'll give you a call once I know more. And I meant it about calling me if you want me to look at her again."

Her smile was genuine this time. "I appreciate that. Really."

And with that, Sebastien sucked down a

quick breath and headed on his way, refusing to give in to the urge to glance back at her as he did.

The second he disappeared around the corner, Rachel slumped against the wall for a second or two, trying to slow her pounding heart. What was it about that man that got her wound up whenever she saw him?

Who was she kidding? It was the way he'd carried her into the resort's overwater cabana a year ago, her legs wrapped around his waist. The way he'd dumped her onto that bed, looking at her as if he couldn't wait to devour her...

Her eyes fluttered shut as memories crashed like ocean waves, drenching her to the skin. She straightened. It was the humidity. It had to be. Besides, what was she doing thinking about him when she needed to get back in the room with Claire?

When her daughter had woken up this morning with a slight fever and a visible swelling on her neck, it had dropped Rachel's heart into her stomach. It bothered her how Claire had acted with him. She'd always been an optimistic child. But when she'd looked for his approval after getting her blood drawn, Rachel had instinctively shifted into protective-mama-bear mode. Claire had never had any contact with her biological father, and even though it made no sense, Rachel feared her being hurt by men. It probably stemmed from her own hurt at being abandoned, but it was hard not to be overprotective. She was sure Sebastien had probably noticed. But she couldn't help it.

Just like she couldn't help that after six years of her daughter's perfect health, Rachel's thoughts immediately ran back toward that first diagnosis of cancer the second Claire felt ill.

She went back into the room. Before she could think of anything to say, Claire took one look at her face and rolled her eyes. "I'm fine, Mom. Really. Did Seb leave already?"

She let herself relax for the first time today. "He did. He had other patients to see."

Which was true, right? He'd said he needed to see if Dr. Rogan had other patients for him to see. "Let's head home. I'll drop you off first, then I'll get us something to eat. Anything special that you want?"

"A mango?"

That made Rachel smile. "A mango. Really?"

"I love them."

They didn't have mangoes where they'd lived in Wisconsin. Or at least nothing like they had in Taurati. Fortunately, she could pick some up at one of the street vendors not far from their apartment. They carried everything from fruits and vegetables to woven baskets. There was a fish market near there as well, so maybe she'd swing by and grab something for dinner. Claire loved the fish on the island.

"Okay, a mango it is. Get dressed so I can get you home."

Claire got up and picked up her clothes, giving her mom a look.

"Oh, okay." She turned her back on her daughter so she could change.

Her daughter was turning into a teenager, and there were days it showed. She pushed back from time to time, which she never had done when she was younger.

Rachel been reluctant to take the job in Taurati at first, because of her daughter's childhood diagnosis, but Claire had talked her into it, saying after being tied to a hospital in the States for the better part of a year doing treatments, followed by periodic scans for years afterward, she wanted to see as many things as the world had to offer. That had made Rachel's decision for her. And it seemed to be the right one, drawing them closer as they struggled to learn a new way of life. But those first days had been hard.

When her mom had come to visit a month after their arrival on the island, saying she wanted to spend time alone with her granddaughter and insisting Rachel take a week for herself and explore the island, she knew exactly why the suggestion had been made. The anniversary of Claire's cancer diagnosis had been nearing, and Rachel always got maudlin, fighting not to smother her daughter with attention and hugs, which only reminded Claire of all she'd been through. Her mom had been right.

They'd compromised on three days rather than a whole week. Rachel ended up not spending that time on the go but opting for a period of quiet reflection at one of the overwater bungalows at a nearby resort. With its thatched roof and dreamy views, it was a tropical paradise.

Never in her wildest dreams had she imagined sitting on a private deck, dangling her feet in the water while colorful fish swam laps around them. It was the perfect place to consider how lucky she was to still have her daughter. To be able to watch her grow up. The magical oasis had probably bewitched her thinking. Because when she was asked if she was okay with being seated at the table of another patron in the resort's packed dining room, she'd said yes.

In more ways than one. Because the occupant of that other table had been none other than the hospital's hunky pediatrician. The outcome of that meeting had been very different than it was today. Because it had been the anniversary of Claire's cancer diagnosis, and she'd been all caught up in her emotions. Her encounter with Seb, and their fun—and very sexy—back-and-forth banter had led to an equally sexy night in her bungalow. The perfect outlet for her churning emotions. At least she'd thought so at the time. The tattoo of a sea turtle on his left shoulder with word *Bleu* scrawled in the middle of it had fascinated her. Was it a reference to the sea life and the gorgeous blue waters of his homeland?

"All done."

Claire's voice pulled her from her thoughts. They went out to the car and, after arriving at the apartment, Rachel saw her daughter inside before taking off on foot to the market. Once there, she picked up several mangoes, a melon and some veggies, then hurried to the fish market. She arrived back home to find Claire flopped on the couch, back in her pj's. A frisson of alarm went through her. "Are you feeling worse?"

"No, but it's Saturday, and I don't have school. I just changed back, since you won't let me do anything with my friends. Right?"

"Right. Not until we know what we're dealing with."

Claire gave a dramatic sigh that made her

smile. Her daughter was definitely an extrovert, unlike her mom, who had to be more intentional in talking to people, due to her job. But she was glad at how easily her girl could make friends.

Except when it came to Sebastien, evidently, since she'd ushered him out of the room as soon as she got a chance. But their conversation in that hallway had shaken her up almost as much as it had in that restaurant a year ago. She'd found herself reading something into almost everything he said.

She smiled to take the sting out of her earlier words. "Well, you're negative for the flu and COVID, so there's that. Sebas—er, Dr. Deslaurier said he'd call as soon as the mono test comes back. It should be anytime now."

Her daughter's head cocked. "I told you you were overreacting. *Seb* doesn't seem worried at all."

Seb. Great. Claire seemed to relish saying the man's name, putting special emphasis on it. She should have objected when the pediatrician had offered it up. But she hadn't. And now it was too late, evidently. Her worry had superseded everything else.

They had both tiptoed around the reason for Rachel's worry, but they both knew exactly what it was about. Knew exactly what she was afraid of, even six years after Claire had finished with her treatments.

Rachel wondered if her daughter knew just how terrified she was every time she had a little cough or a sore throat. Probably. But tenderness in the lymph nodes in her neck was what had set them on that crazy journey of infusions and tests in the first place.

Claire had been one of the lucky ones. There were so many children who weren't. Rachel had seen it with her own eyes through her job. The offer to work in a smaller hospital on the island of Taurati had been a balm to her soul, since her job in Wisconsin had been at a teaching hospital with a huge oncology department. Each child who came through with cancer was like a knife to her heart.

She decided to shift the subject from cancer… or Seb. "How's your French and Tahitian coming?"

One thing she hadn't thought about was the fact that they would both be learning two other languages simultaneously.

"I would say better than yours, but that doesn't sound very nice, does it?"

Rachel grinned and mimicked her daughter's playful tone. "I would say no, it doesn't, but that it's probably true."

Fortunately Taurati had a vibrant tourist industry, so English was widely spoken. Even her encounters with Sebastien had taken place in her heart language, except for those sexy muttered phrases here and there in that hut.

Which she was not going to think about again. Or about the pediatrician's French accent, which was almost as smoking hot as he was. From what Sebastien had said the few times they'd actually spoken about things other than work, she knew his mom was Tahitian and his dad was French. He'd grown up in the islands and had lived in Taurati for the last five years. There'd been murmurs around the nurses' stations about something bad that had happened in his past, but normally those conversations took place in a language other than English, and Rachel tried not to translate them in her head. Once she heard his name mentioned, she did her best to tune the speaker out. The less she knew about him, the better. Because her reaction to him when she didn't even know him? Well, it was electric. And oh, so dangerous.

Even in hospital hallway, when her sick child had been mere footsteps away, she'd had a hard time not absorbing every syllable he said and letting them linger in her head.

"Let me throw together something to eat and then we can watch a movie." She held up her bag. "And the mangoes look out of this world today."

"Yum, thanks."

Rachel went into the kitchen and cut up some of the fruit and then made a light salad and grilled the fish. It was hot enough outside today that the air-conditioning was having trouble keeping up, so something light seemed like the order of the day. Besides, walking home in the oppressive heat had taken a lot out of her.

Or was it due to the playful banter with Sebastien? *Not going there. Not right now.*

When she had their plates ready, she walked into the other room. "Do you want to eat here? Or at the dining room table?" A table that consisted of an ancient round slab of wood and some whitewashed chairs. Rachel loved the charm of it.

"Sofa, for sure."

"Okay, but just for tonight."

Handing Claire a plate, she settled in and turned the television on, choosing a romantic comedy that her daughter said she wanted. Romantic comedy. Well, Rachel's love live was certainly a comedy, but the romantic part? Nope. Not in a long while. Claire's father had skipped out while she'd still been a baby, saying he wasn't ready to be a father. And in her daughter's twelve years, Rachel had had exactly two encounters with men, one of which had been with Sebastien, and surely you couldn't even count that.

Oh, it counted. It definitely counted.

But it was up to her to make sure that their time together stayed firmly entrenched in the past. For everyone's sake. But most importantly Claire's. There was no way she was going to let someone into her daughter's life only to have him walk back out of it again. Been there, done that. The only good part was that Claire didn't remember the pain of her biological dad leaving. But she was definitely old enough to be hurt by something like that now. And the way she'd taken to Sebastien had unnerved Rachel.

Her daughter had enough emotional scars. For that matter, so did she. She was not looking to add to that number.

What she was going to do first was make sure her daughter was okay physically. Then she was going to bury her own heart so deep that nothing or no one would be able to find it. With that decided, she threw herself into watching the movie, trying to enjoy every second she got to spend with her daughter, knowing Claire was growing up way too fast. That was evident in her not wanting her mom to see her change clothes.

She put her free arm around Claire and gave her a quick squeeze. "Love you, kiddo."

Claire looked at her. "I know. Love you, too."

And when her phone rang toward the end of the movie, she glanced down and saw that it was the hospital. Forcing back sentimental tears from the movie they were watching, she took a deep breath and hoped her voice wouldn't shake when she answered.

"Hello?"

"Hi, Rachel, it's Seb."

Seb. Her eyes closed, and she prayed this was the news she wanted to hear.

"The test results?"

"Yes. It's definitely not mono."

Her fingers dug into the arm of the sofa even as she finished up the call, thanking him.

Claire was looking at her with a weird expression. "What is it?"

"It's good news. You don't have mono."

It was strange that good news could also be bad. Very bad.

Because if Claire didn't have mono…what did she have?

CHAPTER TWO

"THERE'S A PROBLEM on the beach."

Rachel looked up at one of the other nurses, who was just putting down a phone. "What is it?"

"Possible drowning victim." Her colleague called out to Seb, who was just exiting a room. "Can you and Rachel run down to the beach out front and help with a kid who's been pulled from the water? Lifeguard is administering CPR but doesn't want to stop to carry the child up the beach to Hospitalier."

There was no time for thought, no time for wondering if she could hand the case over to someone else. She glanced at Sebastien, who was quicker on his feet than she was.

"Let's go."

Grabbing the medical kit that the nurse held out, they headed to the door, Sebastien calling back, "Have them bring a gurney to the edge of the boardwalk so we can use an ambu bag during transport."

"Already on it," said the nurse, phone in her hand.

Rachel raced to the door with Sebastien, a million thoughts and procedures racing through her head.

There was a plank boardwalk at the end of the parking lot that led from the hospital down to the beach. Normally it was used by hospital staff to go out and spend their breaks in one of the colorful beach chairs that the facility placed down there for family and friends. The trained lifeguard was also an employee of the hospital.

Rachel had spent some time down there with Claire, but this was the first time she'd had to rush there to help someone.

As they made the hundred-yard trek over the boards, a stand of thatched buildings on stilts in the water a good distance down the beach caught her eye. They were similar to the ones at the resort where she'd stayed. Rented out as hotel rooms to tourists. Rachel had had visions of paddling a long board out from one of them. Instead, she'd brought Seb back to the one she'd rented, forever changing what she thought about when she looked at the structures.

That was soon forgotten as she caught sight

of the desperate life-and-death battle being waged just above the shoreline.

"Oh, God, oh, God, *oh, God*!"

She wasn't sure whether the keening cries coming from a woman who knelt next to the lifeguard were a desperate plea or a horrified epithet, but they were going to haunt her for a while.

Seb reached them first, with Rachel just a second or two behind. He touched the lifeguard's back. "We'll take over and you can fill us in."

The man slid out of the way, his breath coming in heavy gasps as Sebastien handed her the ambu bag while he quickly checked for signs of breathing and a pulse.

"Nothing...yet."

She had a feeling the last part of the sentence was added for the woman who'd cried out a few second earlier. But she couldn't worry about that right now.

Fitting the mouthpiece over the child—a little girl, who couldn't be more than five or six—she started respirations while Seb did compressions.

Before the lifeguard could say anything, the woman grabbed the child's hand as tears fell freely down her face. "A wave grabbed her from me. I couldn't hold on. I couldn't. I tried!"

The man who'd been doing compressions nodded at her. "I know you did." He then turned to Seb. "The wave knocked the child over, and I lost sight of her for a second. I went in. It took me about three minutes to find her and get her to shore."

Three minutes. Three minutes in which precious oxygen had been cut off from the girl's brain. The waters here were warm—they weren't like the frigid lakes in Wisconsin, where the cold could slow down body functions and provide more time for rescues.

Seb didn't answer, continuing to count compressions, but it was obvious he was listening, his glance coming up and spearing hers for a second. And the flash of pain she saw in his eyes…

Of course Rachel was just as anxious to revive this little girl as he was, but the look on Sebastien's face shocked her. Normally the pediatrician's eyes were cloaked with some kind of secrecy that she couldn't decipher. Not that she tried. Or wanted to. Not since that night he'd whispered into her ear, the hot and sexy syllables needing no translation. From that time on, however, there'd been no break in his steely demeanor. And she was glad of it.

Especially after seeing what she'd just witnessed in his eyes.

What had happened to him?

She remembered the whispers among the staff. Maybe she should have listened a little closer.

About three minutes went by as they worked in silence, then the child moved, her hands opening and closing. As if mentally synced, she and Seb both rolled the girl onto her side, where with a convulsive heave of her chest, a blast of water shot from her mouth. She started coughing.

A shout from the side pulled Rachel's attention to the boardwalk. Two hospital orderlies stood there with a gurney.

The lifeguard had to physically hold the distraught woman back to keep her from crawling over and crowding them.

Maybe the words shouted earlier really had been a prayer, because by some miracle, the child's eyes fluttered open, the blue of them brighter to Rachel than the sun.

Her gaze swung over the people gathered around her. "Mommy?"

The lifeguard let the woman go, and she leaned down and cradled the child's head, raining kisses and tears onto her forehead. "Oh, baby… Thank God."

Seb interrupted. "We still need to get her to the hospital. What's her name?"

"Sharon." The woman's voice caught on a sob before coming back again. "Her name is Sharon."

"Let's get Sharon on the gurney, and we'll get her checked out."

"Thank you. Thank you so much. All of you."

Seb's face visibly tightened. "Don't thank us just yet. We still need to check her over and make sure there's no more water in her lungs."

He climbed to his feet and swung Sharon effortlessly into his arms and strode with her to the gurney waiting a short distance away. The sight of him holding that little girl made Rachel's throat tighten.

The girl twisted, looking back. "Mommy!"

"I'm right here, honey."

Now that the urgency of the situation had faded a bit, Rachel stopped to speak to the lifeguard. "You saved her life. Thank you."

The young man, who was probably not yet thirty, nodded, dragging his fingers through his hair. "Hell, I thought for a few minutes…" His voice took on a rough edge before fading away.

Rachel knew exactly what it was like after that rush of adrenaline leached away, leaving a big hole of nothingness. She reached over and squeezed his hand. "I think we all did. But you didn't give up. That's why she's alive."

Seb's voice came back to her as the gurney moved up the walkway. "Rachel. Could you grab the ambu bag on your way in?"

"Yep. On my way." With an apologetic glance at the lifeguard, she let go of him and smiled. "Well, thanks again."

"Can you let me know how she does?"

"I'll ask her mom if it's okay." With that, she grabbed the lifesaving device, turned and hurried up the pathway, having to jog to catch up with the little group.

Little Sharon was talking to her mom, asking why she was crying.

"Because I'm just so happy, baby."

"Happy I'm okay?"

"Yes, that's exactly it."

The tightness in Rachel's throat moved to her eyes. She knew exactly what it was like to realize your child was going to be okay after fearing they were going to die. The rush of relief that made your legs weak and your words fail.

The day she'd gotten the news that Claire had cancer had been one of the worst of her life. And she'd had absolutely no one to lean on but her parents. She'd wrestled with whether or not she should try to find Roy, her ex, and let him know, but he'd been pretty adamant that he didn't want to be a father. And he'd never once contacted them, even though Rachel and

Claire still lived in the same town in which their daughter was born.

Her daughter. Roy might have been there for her birth, but he'd become distant and moody, seeming totally put out when Claire cried. She should have seen the split coming, but she'd been so wrapped up in the birth and lack of sleep that big swaths of time became a blur.

Claire had asked about her father a couple of times over the years, but so far Rachel had glossed over the fact that her ex hadn't wanted anything to do with her. But at some point, her daughter was going to want to know more. She might even want to try to find her father. And when that happened, Rachel would have to do her best to prepare her for what might not be a rosy reunion.

At the top of the boardwalk, Sebastien gave her a look that made her frown.

"Is she okay?" The ambu bag was still in her left hand, she realized, but there was something about the way his eyes jerked back to their patient that made her frown deepen. As if he were worried more than he was letting on.

"I hope so. We'll need to get her to radiology to check her lungs. Good job, though."

"Thanks." Trying not to let the words cause her heart to jump, she turned her attention back to her patient, getting the child to smile at a story about Claire's first trip to the ocean. And when they reached the door to the hospital, she was glad that her interaction with Sebastien was almost at an end. Because his voice made her want to hang on to his every word. And that was a path that was rife with danger. She knew that from experience.

The doors opened with a whisper of sound as they all went through them. Seb wasn't sure what was wrong with him. As he'd seen the child lying on the beach, her lips taking on a bluish tinge, an image of him standing over Bleu's lifeless body had come back to him. Layla had tried to pull him away, to give him some comfort, but he'd just brushed her off, telling her he was fine when he obviously wasn't.

It reminded him of the lifeguard having to pull the girl's mother away. He thought Rachel had noticed at first, but thankfully she'd seemed oblivious to what was running through his mind.

His and Layla's relationship had started off hot and heavy. But physical attraction and the hormones of youth had rushed them past the important parts of courtship. The parts of getting to know each other. Of learning what caring and commitment truly meant. After their baby died…well, there'd been nothing of substance left between them. He'd been left feeling…empty. It was no wonder she'd walked away from him not long afterward. Just one more person gone from his life.

The emergency room staff was in ready mode, and they went into action as he concentrated on sending out requests for Sharon's blood ox to be monitored and asked them to page whoever the on-call pulmonologist was.

"Are you going to keep her?" The girl's mom, who'd told him her name was Marie, still looked beyond worried. Beyond scared.

"I'd like her to stay overnight, just to keep an eye on her, okay? And I've called for a lung specialist to have a look at her." He didn't want to scare Sharon's mom with possibilities of dry drowning—where lungs became inflamed by the sudden introduction of water into them. Even after the water was gone, the inflammatory process sometimes continued, filling the lungs with fluid produced by the body itself.

"Can I stay with her?"

"I think that can be arranged. Let's get those bloods drawn, and then we'll get her into a room." He forced a smile. "I think she's going to sleep well tonight after all this excitement."

Marie immediately relaxed, and it made Sebastien tense even further. This happened time and time again with the family of his patients, and he'd had to learn to be very careful with his words. Sharon was out of immediate danger, but outcomes rarely came with a guarantee. One of Bleu's doctors had been brusque and cold, as if his son's life—or death—was of no concern to him. Questions were met with irritation and dismissal. Seb had vowed he would not be like that. He would truly invest in his patients' lives—welcome any and all questions. But, at times, it led to a type of emotional exhaustion that was hard to shake.

"That's the kind of excitement I can do without," Sharon's mom said with a smile.

"I agree. Me, too."

Rachel was hanging back a bit, the breathing device clutched to her chest. She looked a little harried. Maybe Claire was worse. He excused himself and then went over to her.

"Are you okay?"

"I think so. It was touch and go there for a while."

"Yes, it was." He paused. "Is the lifeguard okay? I saw you talking to him."

"He's kind of shell-shocked." She crossed her arms over her chest. "Just like we get after a crisis has passed, when we're trying to find our balance."

Was that even possible? Had he found his

balance after Bleu's death? He wasn't quite sure, even after all this time.

A shadow in her expression made him wonder if she was talking about Sharon or if she was thinking about her own daughter. Or was it that emotional exhaustion he'd thought about moments earlier? Before he could work it out, her chin gave a dangerous wiggle, lips thinning as if she was working to hold back her emotions. "Hey, let's take a break and go outside for a few minutes."

She sighed out a huge breath. "Thanks. I don't know what's wrong with me."

"It's okay. I'll be right back." He went over to the staff and let them know he'd be outside in the courtyard area for a few minutes if they needed him. "Let me know when the pulmonologist arrives."

Once outside, he led the way to a concrete bench not far from the boardwalk. Facing the ocean, it was close enough that the spicy breeze from the water reached them, while far enough that they were away from sunbathers or the lifeguard, who looked like he'd resumed his post.

Finding his own balance?

He motioned for Rachel to sit down and joined her, watching as she sucked down a quick breath, her brown eyes not quite landing on any one thing.

"Just take a moment or two to let it run its course."

"To let what run its course?"

She was pretending. It was there in the fingers fidgeting in her lap, the tight set to her shoulders that said she was still making an effort to contain something. How many times had he done that same thing? Pretended not to feel. Not to care. And when his fiancée had left, hadn't he worked even harder at it? He still did—in his private life, anyway. The funny thing was he was more open with his patients than he was with friends and family.

"The energy. Or adrenaline, as you said about the lifeguard. Whether that child lived or died, we did our best by her—you know that, right?"

Was this about Sharon? Or was he lecturing himself about Bleu's death?

"I do know. But I'm very grateful for this outcome instead of what could have happened."

No one knew that better than Sebastien, who'd seen firsthand what the alternative was.

"How is Claire, by the way? Feeling any better?"

Two days had passed since he'd examined Rachel's daughter. He hadn't seen her in that time to ask about her. He'd since asked that all other tests be sent to Dr. Rogan, since he was

Claire's primary care physician. Could she have gotten bad news? Maybe that was playing a role in her shakiness today. Hell, he hoped not.

"She is. Dr. Rogan called me. The diagnosis ended up being lymphadenopathy."

"Caused by?" Lymphadenopathy was the technical term for an enlargement of the lymph nodes. It could be caused by anything from tuberculosis to mono—to cancer.

Rachel gave a shrug. "They think from the cold she'd had a few days earlier. Since it's viral, it just has to run its course, which it seems to be doing. The swelling is much less pronounced today."

He hadn't realized he was holding his breath until she said *less pronounced*. He released it in a rush, wincing at how loud it sounded to his own ears. "That's great. I know you were worried."

She tilted her head. "Having kids is hard. Worry kind of comes with the territory."

The inference was *if you had children, you'd understand*.

He wouldn't have corrected her, even if she'd said the words out loud. His private life was his own concern, not hers.

And yet, he'd just sat here and asked about hers.

So he just said, "Yes, it does. I see that every

day in the parents of my patients. Anyway, I'm glad she's feeling better."

"Thank you." Her eyes held his for a minute, as if probing for something.

It made him haul himself to his feet. "Well, I probably need to get back and see how Sharon's doing. Why don't you stay here and decompress for a bit?"

"No, I'm fine." She stood as well. "Besides, I want to see how she is, too. And if I had to decompress every time there was an emergency, I wouldn't be a very good nurse, would I? I think it just hit me because Claire was about this age when I got the news that she was sick. Really sick."

Bleu had still been an infant when he and Layla realized his eyes had stopped tracking their movements. It had taken a mere MRI to bring them the news no parent ever wants to hear.

"I can understand that." And he did. Babies who presented with neurological symptoms did the same to him. And the one case of brain cancer he'd diagnosed had caused him to take a few days of personal time. But he'd gotten through it.

Rachel would get through this as well. And in the end, she'd go home to be with her child.

Would be able to hug her tight and assure her that all was right with the world.

And it was. With their little piece of it, anyway. But there were never any guarantees in this life.

She nodded toward the hospital. "Shall we?"

"Yep."

With that, they made their way back to the hospital, and he told himself that the next time someone seemed stressed out by a case, he was going to let them handle it in their own way, without any input or interference from him.

It would be easier for that person. And it would certainly be a whole lot easier for him.

CHAPTER THREE

SEBASTIEN WALKED PAST the picture of his son, just as he did every morning. Except normally he gave it a passing glance before moving on with his day. This time, however, he picked it up and looked at it, studying the curly brown hair and tiny lips. Maybe because of his encounter with Rachel yesterday. He wasn't sure why, but he'd had a hard time sleeping last night. And when he had fallen into slumber, he'd had dreams of Bleu being carried away by ocean currents while he'd trudged through the surf, unable to reach him.

The dreams he understood. They were caused by little Sharon's near drowning. Fortunately, she'd been fine the rest of the night at the hospital, and she was set to be released.

Today was a new day. For that he was glad. He looked again at his son's image.

The pregnancy had been unexpected, but he'd been prepared to marry Layla and make a family with her and their child. He'd been young and idealistic and had even managed to convince himself that he loved her. All would be right with the world as long as he believed it was so. But, of course, it hadn't been, and after Bleu died, there'd been a thread of relief when Layla walked out.

Maybe it was because he'd needed to grieve Bleu's death privately, but he didn't think that was the entire reason. And despite any regret he may have had about Layla's absence, it just drove home the fact that people left. Whether they wanted to or not.

Afraid he might somehow forget his son, he'd impulsively walked into a tattoo parlor a few weeks later and had Bleu's name and favorite toy tattooed on his left shoulder. Of course, he never forgot him, but he did forget about the ink on his body most days. But when he'd done another impulsive thing and slept with Rachel, she'd reminded him of exactly why he avoided relationships. He'd been sitting on the bed reaching down for his clothing when gentle fingers had touched his shoulder and he realized what she'd found. A spear shafted straight to his heart as he relived those terrible days leading to Bleu's death.

He couldn't afford another accidental pregnancy, and despite the protection he'd used, a sense of fear oozed through him right after their encounter. He'd wanted to ask her about it later on when he saw her at the hospital a few weeks after their night together, but he couldn't bring himself to. She'd tell him if it somehow happened, wouldn't she?

And she'd acted so chilly toward him after that night, he didn't think she'd welcome any probing questions about her fertility.

Hell, even thinking about it in those terms made him cringe.

Maybe the tattoo was a good thing. The few times he'd slept with someone, there'd always been *that* question—the one about the meaning of that tat. It would either jerk him out of the moment or remind him of his silent vow not to become a father again. Bleu would keep him on the straight and narrow, even from the grave. Strangely, Rachel had not asked about it. She'd simply traced gentle fingertips across it and left it at that. But that soft touch had left its mark. He could still feel it in unguarded moments. Or whenever he saw her at work.

He set the picture back down on the end table, swearing he felt a sharp twinge in his shoulder as he did. Maybe there really was an afterlife and that was his son's way of communicating with him.

"Wish you were still here, kid."

Sighing, he went into the bathroom and looked himself in the face. Thirty-five years had not been kind to him. There were gray strands threaded through black hair that was a little too long. He swept it back off his forehead. He always seemed to go too long in between cuts. Maybe because of that huge mirror in most salons and the awkward conversations with strangers who inevitably asked about family relationships. And kids.

How did you answer that question?

He did have a kid. But to speak of Bleu in the present tense seemed like a lie. But to tell the truth? That was even more awkward and usually resulted in shocked silence, followed by swift backtracking and murmurs of sympathy. And it all happened in sight of that mirror.

Yeah. Well, his hair would survive another couple of weeks before he went through that again. Right?

With that, he brushed his teeth and shaved, having taken a shower before going to bed. It was a habit now. Because you never knew when the phone could ring in the middle of the night with an emergency case.

He still got a Christmas card from Bleu's maternal grandparents every year. And almost every year, they updated him on their daughter's life. She still wasn't married. Still didn't have any other kids. It was almost as if they were trying to get him to call her. He wouldn't.

He realized now that their reasons for getting married would have made for a difficult union at best.

Besides, his life wasn't in Tahiti anymore. It was here in Taurati. And if Layla's parents wanted more grandchildren, they needed to look to someone else. Because it wouldn't be him. There were too many might-have-beens juxtaposed with what actually was. Not a good basis for marriage or anything else.

And that held true for friendships as well. His conversation with Rachel yesterday had exposed the same glaring contrasts between their situations. But he could see it a little more clearly now. That while Rachel might feel fortunate to still have her daughter, that clawing fear of loss was never far from the surface. Sebastien had just assumed that it went away with time. But evidently not.

He wasn't sure he could handle going through that every time he faced a difficult case.

Not even if it meant having Bleu still here with him?

Well, that was different. Of course he wished his son had lived. The difference was, Claire wasn't his. And he wasn't going to willingly walk into a situation where he would be reminded day in and day out what the future might hold.

Selfish? Absolutely. But wasn't self-preservation a selfish instinct at its core?

That hadn't stopped him from sleeping with someone who'd had a child, though. But he hadn't known at the time about Claire's cancer. If he had, things might have ended very differently that night. Instead, they had indulged in some sexy give-and-take banter that reminded him how fun it used to be to do that. She'd been new to the island, and he'd offered to show her a few sights. And she'd shown him a few as well—like the interior of her overwater bungalow, where they'd fallen into bed together.

The next morning, she'd traced his shoulder. The memory sent a shudder through him.

Damn. He swung away from the mirror and finished dressing. This was why he didn't connect with people, even in friendship. It was why, despite his years in Taurati, real friends were few and far between. And all the ones he did have were colleagues at work.

He wasn't actually on call today, but most mornings found him in his office doing paperwork. His office was safe. Private. And it was where he liked to pass the time.

To avoid taking part in the world at large?

To avoid another incident like the one with Rachel a year ago?

Probably. But it was what it was.

He caught a taxi and headed to the hospital. The second he pushed through the doors, his phone pinged. Weird. Almost everyone knew that Tuesdays were his day off. He glanced down at the screen. It was from the hospital administrator.

Hey, are you here yet?

His lips curved. That was the one downside to being so predictable. Neves was one of those few friends, and the man pretty much knew exactly where he could find Seb. The administrator was sharp and was very good at his job, which was to keep the hospital running well, heading off problems before anyone even knew there was one.

He texted back. Just arriving.

Can you come up?

He sighed before responding. He'd been looking forward to some alone time after his thoughts this morning. But it wasn't like he could just refuse.

On my way.

Neves Bouchet's office was in the same fourth floor wing as his and most of the other permanent physicians' spaces. Waiting for the elevator around the corner, his eye caught sight of the ocean a short way from the hospital. Framed by green palm fronds and white beaches, the calm azure color of the water was as alluring on Taurati as it was on the other islands of French Polynesia. Except he saw it so often that sometimes he had to remind himself of its beauty. His time in medical school in France had given him a new appreciation of the islands where he'd been born.

The elevator doors opened, and he was dumped onto the fourth floor. Rounding the corner, he pushed through the glass door to Neves's waiting area. He frowned when he spied Rachel in one of the chairs. He glanced around. No one else was here.

Hell, he hoped this wasn't about what had happened between them last year. In all honesty, he'd been waiting for that to catch up with him. But after a year?

You're being paranoid, Seb.

They'd both been consenting adults who'd agreed to remain mum about the night they'd shared. Not that the hospital really had any rules against colleagues sleeping together, although the unspoken consensus was that it could be a sticky situation. But it evidently worked for some. There was at least one pair of surgeons at Centre Hospitalier who were married. And his and Rachel's encounter had only been one night long.

Rachel didn't even look at him. Dressed in a gauzy white skirt and a blouse that was as blue as the ocean, she looked almost as inviting as the warm currents a short distance away. And when she crossed her legs—that slow slide of calf over calf was reminiscent of... He swallowed. *Okay, don't go there.*

But at odds with his thoughts were the tense lines in her face and her refusal to glance his way. It couldn't be a coincidence that she was here. Did she know why they'd been summoned? Was this about the girl at the beach yesterday?

He glanced at Neves's administrative assistant, who must have guessed his thoughts, because she nodded. "He hoped you were in the building so he could meet with you both together."

His eyes went back to Rachel before returning to the desk. "About?"

"Hey, I just work here." Cécile raised her hands, palms out, in a way that said she had no idea why they were here. And he couldn't very well ask Rachel if she knew. Not in front of Neves's assistant.

Cécile picked up her office phone and murmured something into it. Then she looked up. "You can go on in."

When no one moved, she grinned. "Both of you."

Sebastien waited for Rachel to stand and then motioned for her to go ahead of him. It was the polite thing to do, but it would also help him put a halt to his racing thoughts. If Neves wanted to talk about possible rumors or innuendos surrounding their night together, he wasn't sure what he was going to say. And if it was something else entirely?

Well, it would be a relief.

Rachel ducked through the door, and he followed her.

Neves stood to greet them. "Hi, guys. Thanks for taking some time out from your day. I have something I want to discuss, but I'd rather it not go any farther than this room at the moment."

Merde. Maybe there was something floating around the hospital after all.

Rachel beat him to the punch. "I'm not sure I understand, Neves."

Although Neves was technically an internal medicine doctor, once he took over the hospi-

tal's administrative duties, he'd stopped prac-
ticing medicine. He said it was because of how
much time the position took, but he also said it
could give the impression of favoritism if one
patient got resources that another was denied.

"Sit, please."

There were only two chairs across from the
desk, so there was no option but to sit next to
her. Seb hoped to hell his afternoon went better than his morning was going so far. Or yesterday, for that matter. Working so closely with
Rachel on that case had brought back some
memories of its own. And he'd been surprised
by the easy rhythm between them as they
worked to resuscitate Sharon. He didn't want
easy between them. He wanted their interactions to be damned hard. So hard that he kept
avoiding her like he had for the past year.

He dropped into his chair and looked at the
administrator. "What's this about, Neves?"

The man looked down at some papers on his
desk before lifting his head to look from one
to the other. "Did either of you catch the news
today?"

Seb attempted a smile. "Not today. Is Centre
Hospitalier on lockdown or something?" Kind
of a stupid question, since he'd just walked right
through the front doors.

"Not yet."

What the hell? Was there some communicable disease swirling around? COVID had done a number on them a while back. The last thing they needed was something new on the horizon. "So we might have to go on lockdown? Why?"

"You haven't seen the weather reports?"

Sebastien remembered thinking the good old South Pacific looked pretty calm today. And the sun was a big hot orb in the sky, just like it was most days.

Rachel cocked her head. "No. What about them?"

"There's an area out there that could become worrisome if it develops any further."

"An area, as in a hurricane? I thought those didn't happen here."

Neves nodded. "They don't normally. And cyclones, as they're called in this part of the world, are rare in Polynesia. But they're certainly not unheard-of."

The last major cyclone to strike the area was named Wasa-Arthur, if he remembered right. But that had been decades ago. Surely if there was one off the coast, he would have heard about it by now. "What does any of that have to do with us?"

Neves leaned forward. "Again, I don't want any of this leaving this room." His voice lowered. "Rachel guessed correctly. There's a low-pressure system out there."

"A low-pressure system." He frowned. "This is the time for them. Is it threatening the island?" November through April was normally when cyclones formed in this part of the world.

"Right now, I'm choosing to err on the side of preparedness."

"What does that mean, exactly?" Rachel's voice slid past him.

"It means I would like you two to go over hospital protocols and make sure everything is up-to-date and in place. I normally have Laurence and Britan do that this time of year, even if there's no system forming out there, but they're expecting and I don't want to put any more on them."

Laurence and Britan were the married surgeons he'd thought about this morning. "I didn't know they were expecting."

"I found out about it last month. But she's had a couple of spikes in her blood pressure. Nothing serious, but Laurence came in after hearing about the depression and asked if they could be replaced as the cyclone committee this year."

Committee. Okay, so that meant multiple people, right?

"Can't other members of the committee pick up the slack?"

Neves laughed. "If there were any other members, then yes. But they worked well together and always got the job done. And since you're here most days, even on your days off, Seb, I thought you could step in." His glance moved to Rachel. "And as one of the newest members of our medical staff, I thought you might like to get an insider's view of how things work at the hospital during emergencies. Unless there's some reason you'd rather not be a part of a working committee."

Several seconds went by with a series of expressions winding across her face. Consternation. Tension. Dismay. And then relief.

Relief?

Maybe, like him, she'd thought the administrator had called her in for a completely different reason. Maybe they could make this quick if they were stuck working together.

Rachel shrugged. "No, it's fine as long as I can help with it during most of my on-duty hours. I have a daughter at home."

"Of course. And if you're swamped with cases, those come first, obviously. Just in the quieter times of the day. Maybe an hour or two here and there. You two figure out when you can meet."

And hour or two? Here and there? A lot could happen within that set of parameters.

His brain swore at him again. No. Nothing was going to happen. Other than what Neves had asked them to do: review protocol.

"It shouldn't take long, then."

Neves sent his gaze Seb's way. "However long it takes for that system to burn itself out or head in a different direction. I don't want what happened in '91 to catch us unprepared again. Our hospital's power grid was taken out with that one, resulting in the deaths of two patients."

Sebastien remembered hearing about that. "I'm not sure how we can prevent something like that."

"I know you can't make any guarantees. But you can go through the evacuation procedures if it comes to that and oversee their implementation. It's what Laurence and Britan were charged with. I thought if you were both willing…" Neves's voice trailed off.

If Seb said no, his friend would want an explanation—one he was loath to provide. Especially not in front of Rachel.

"I'm fine with it." He looked at Rachel, brows slightly raised in challenge. "How about you?"

"Y-yes, of course. If it will help. My daughter comes first, though. She's just getting over a virus."

"Understood. Bring her to work with you, if it will help."

Oh, hell, no. He and Rachel would have to keep this within the boundaries of work hours. "I'm sure we can get this all done during our scheduled shifts."

He was relieved to see Rachel nod. "Yes, I'm sure we can. Besides, if it's been that long since your last storm, then I'm sure this one will spin out before it even starts. Nothing will happen."

Even before her confident words ended, a low chill slid through Sebastien's veins. She hadn't been here long enough to know what every islander understood from birth. One thing they were careful never to do. One did not challenge their island and expect to walk away unscathed.

He would do well to listen to his own counsel and realize you did not challenge fire and expect to come away with clear lungs and unsinged hands. So if he and Rachel were going to have to work together in a manner that was unlike what they did on a day-to-day basis at the hospital, then he was going to have to be on guard. Each and every hour that they spent together.

* * *

Why her? Why on earth had the hospital administrator chosen her of all people?

He'd already told her. She'd drawn the short straw because she was one of the newer members of Hospitalier's team. Something she wasn't thrilled about at the moment. Especially in light of her shakiness in working with Sebastien yesterday. Her knees had been like rubber. And once they'd handed Sharon off in the hospital, she'd been in danger of falling apart. He'd noticed, inviting her to take a break for a few minutes. Once she realized it would be with him, she should have refused. But to do that would let him know just how uncomfortable she was in his company.

But for the administrator to ask her to help monitor a cyclone?

Which cyclone was she referring to? Sebastien? Or the actual weather pattern?

Right now, it was both. Even sitting beside him for those few minutes in Neves's office had sent her nerves through the roof. In fact, the second Sebastien had walked in the door of the reception area, her senses had gone on high alert, a feeling of doom hanging over her head.

She hadn't been wrong about the doom part. They left the office together, and she couldn't help but ask, "How bad was the storm he was referring to? The one where those patients died?"

"I wasn't on Taurati at the time, but it was bad. I was still a kid, living in Tahiti. It was hit pretty hard, too. But Taurati has fewer resources. Less money."

"Fewer options." She hesitated before asking what was first and foremost on her mind. "How can I get Claire off the island if it looks like it's going to come our way? My mom lives in the States, in Wisconsin."

He looked at her for a long minute. "Let's go get some coffee and talk without worrying about being overheard."

That didn't sound good. Did he think she was being totally selfish for voicing that question and wanted to chastise her in private? Maybe he would be right to.

Would they actually be able to evacuate anyone, or would there be widespread panic that would keep people from getting out? She made a mental note to call her mom as soon as they were done here. Maybe Claire could take a week or two vacation from school and leave before it became necessary. Before there was a crush of people trying to get out.

That made her tense and sent her back to her first question—wasn't she giving herself an unfair advantage that others on the island didn't have?

Maybe Neves had been wrong about choosing her. After all, she and Claire could just slip unnoticed off the island and never come back, and she'd never have to face what the rest of the folks here might have to endure.

She already knew she wasn't going to do that.

If she could do something to help on Taurati, she was going to stay and do it. And if it meant sending Claire away so she could focus on her job, she would. Whatever it took. Even if that entailed working with a man who sent her pulse soaring into the heavens. She just hoped that, unlike Icarus, she stayed well out of the danger zone and made sure her feet weren't too far off the ground. And that her heart didn't venture too close to the sun.

CHAPTER FOUR

OF COURSE SHE was worried about her daughter. He couldn't blame her.

Sebastien opened the door to a nearby coffee shop and found a table in a far corner. When one of the waitstaff came over for their order, he nodded for Rachel to go first, his brows going up when she ordered an espresso.

He wasn't sure what he'd been expecting or why, but he found her order matched what he knew about her. She was straightforward without a lot of artifice. Maybe working with her would have been easier if she were totally fake. That would be easy to resist. But he didn't think she had a fake bone in her body. Not with how quick she was to talk about her daughter's illness. Far from telling him to mind his own business, she'd given him an honest appraisal without hesitation.

That was very different from how begrudging he was with information whenever asked his marital status or whether or not he had kids. But he didn't think that was just about his own comfort. It was awkward for everyone involved when he talked about his son.

Neves knew about Bleu, and so did a few other friends. But for the most part, no one at the hospital had any idea that the baby had ever existed. And on some level, that made him incredibly sad.

He realized the waiter still had his pen poised over his pad.

"Sorry. I'll have a café au lait."

Once the man left, he decided to be blunt. "I don't think either of us knew why Neves wanted to see us this morning. If you feel uncomfortable working with me, I can talk to him and see if—"

"Why would I feel uncomfortable working with you?"

He paused before trying again. "Are you saying you're not?"

Rachel leaned forward with a smile he could only classify as sardonic. "If you're talking about that crazy night a year ago, I'd almost forgotten all about it."

Shock made him sit back...until she laughed and continued, "I'm kidding. Of course it's awkward. But if I let a little awkwardness stand between me and my job, I'd have a hard time working anywhere. Not that I sleep with men I barely know wherever I go."

That made him chuckle, his muscles relaxing en masse. "Okay, now that we've addressed the elephant in the room, let's talk about your daughter."

"Excuse me?"

"I'm referring to getting her off the island if it looks like the pressure system is going to turn into an actual storm."

"I realize how that must have sounded, since so many others don't have the luxury of doing that, and I'm sorry if—"

"It's okay. I understand where you're coming from." His hand touched hers just as the waiter arrived with their coffees, making him pull back. They murmured their thanks, and the man slid away on silent feet.

Taking a bracing sip of his coffee, he tried to banish the sensations that brief touch had caused. Her skin was every bit as soft as he remembered. His brain resurrected memories of rolling her beneath him and making love to her far into the night.

Hmm...not making love. It was sex.

Did it really matter what it was called? The experience had left him unsettled, no matter what label he decided to slap on that night.

Forcing himself to return to the matter at

hand, he responded to her words. "I would do the same if I were in your shoes. It's not just about keeping Claire safe. It's about eliminating distractions that could interfere with what needs to be done."

Distractions. Like innocent touches that brought not-so-innocent reactions?

"That's what I told myself, too. Then I wondered if I was trying to justify myself for even thinking about evacuating her."

"For what it's worth, I think you're right about wanting her off the island if the system looks like it will threaten Taurati. Part of living here means realizing the islands are not exempt from cyclones. But it's also knowing that they are the exception rather than the rule. There are other places that deal with these types of storms on a yearly basis, including parts of the States. We're fortunate enough that they normally veer off in another direction long before they get close to us."

"So when do you suggest I worry?"

"I'll tell you in enough time to arrange it. Before there's widespread panic."

"Thank you." This time it was her fingers that reached across to squeeze his. And there it was again—that immediate sense of wanting to prolong that contact for as long as possible. Before he could act on that thought, she

sat back in her chair. "So what's the first thing
we need to do?"

"Do?"

"As far as making sure the hospital is ready?"

He thought for a second. "Maybe we can
meet in my office as time allows and run
through the stuff that Laurence and Britan
have on file."

"Should we meet with them, too?"

"Maybe. If she's having a tough pregnancy,
though, I don't want to add to their stress levels. But we also may need some insight that we
won't find in the files. I'll feel them out and see
what they think."

Sebastien knew the couple, but he wasn't
close to either one of them. If Laurence had
already asked to be replaced, maybe they would
resent being approached. If so, the other man
could simply say no. But he had a feeling they
would be glad to meet with Seb and Rachel.
They just didn't want to be responsible for the
whole thing, since they were focused on the
health of their child.

"Sounds good. What's your schedule like?"

"I'm actually off today. I just came in because I find it easier to…"

To what? Forget about his son? Forget that
there was a social world out there where people still laughed…still loved? He finished his

sentence with "I find it easier to catch up on paperwork when I'm not treating patients."

"Or dealing with storms?" She smiled when she said it, her demitasse poised in front of her mouth. And when she took that sip, her lips clung to the white porcelain in a way that made his mouth go dry. Right now there was a storm of a completely different type sending gale-force winds through his insides. Only it wasn't a distant threat, like the low-pressure system far offshore. This storm was right on top of him, threatening to whisk any semblance of caution away and fling it so far he'd have a hell of a time finding it again.

So he gripped it tighter and hoped his damn hands didn't lose hold and make him do something he'd regret.

Like he'd done a year ago? When he and Rachel had been glued together on a bed, unable to get enough of each other? Yes. Exactly like that. And he had a feeling if it happened again, it might not be quite as easy to walk away. So he needed to concentrate on what had to be done. Right here. Right now. Starting with what he was about to say.

"Okay, let's get to work on Neves's project."

Sharon was doing fine. By the time Rachel made it back to the hospital, she was afraid maybe the girl would be released before she'd had a chance to say goodbye. But she was still in her room, sitting up in bed. Marie was perched on the mattress next to her, holding her close.

It had been harder than it should have been to put an end to their coffee meeting. Two hours later, Sebastien had been the one to do it, standing and stretching his back, the bottom of his shirt coming up just enough for her to catch a sliver of tanned abdomen. Lord, she'd been done for. Hadn't been able to get out of there fast enough.

Swallowing, she shifted her attention to the bed. "How is she doing?"

"She seems to be no worse for wear, unlike her mother." Marie laughed, but the sound was brittle, like someone who was barely holding things together.

She understood exactly what that was like.

Rachel moved closer to the pair. "I get it. I had a scare with my own daughter several years ago. I wasn't sure how I was going to get through it."

"Your daughter almost drowned, too?"

"No, but she had cancer, and I was afraid she wasn't going to survive."

The young mother's teeth came down on her lip. "But she's okay now?"

"Yes. She's now twelve years old and doing great. I think Sharon is going to do great as well."

"So do I." A masculine voice came from behind her, and Rachel whirled around.

"I—I didn't know you were coming here." She couldn't stop her eyes from sliding to the bottom of his shirt and the area she'd stared at earlier, only to find it firmly covered.

One side of his mouth quirked. "And I didn't know *you* were coming here."

When Marie looked at them funny, Rachel quickly said, "We just came out of a meeting."

"Well, I'm glad you were both able to see her. I'd like to get a picture of you both with her, if I could."

Both of them? As in together? But what could she say? That she didn't want to be in a picture with him?

Seb seemed anything but worried as he smoothly replied, "Of course. We'd be happy to, wouldn't we, Rachel?"

"Yes."

Marie slid off the bed and pulled her phone from her pocket. "Mommy wants to get a picture of you and the doctors, okay?"

Sharon nodded her head and smiled.

Rachel got on one side of the girl, while Sebastien got on the other, both putting their arm around her at the same time. She shivered when his fingertips brushed against her bare arm. He hadn't done it on purpose, but by her reaction, he might as well have.

Damn. Pull yourself together, Rachel.

"Okay, on the count of three."

Sharon's mom counted down, and Rachel forced her lips to stretch in a wide grin that she was pretty sure looked macabre.

"One more." The phone went still for another shot. "Thank you both. For everything."

Rachel moved away so quickly she almost stumbled and had to put a hand on the bed to catch herself.

Girl, you are in trouble.

To cover her mental discomfort, she turned to the girl. "Take care of your mom, okay? You gave her a pretty big scare." She hoped the child understood. While the islanders spoke a combination of Tahitian and French, most also knew some English. She used her broken French to repeat herself. Four years of college French seemed so inadequate for real-life use.

The girl nodded.

Okay, so she'd understood her. That was good.

It might not hurt for her to brush up on the language and use it more. After all, she was living in their country now. So she was going to do it. At least with their younger patients.

She said her goodbyes and slid from the room so she wouldn't have to stay and make any more small talk. She needed to get back to work—and she needed to get away from Seb. Before she embarrassed herself any further.

But no sooner had she exited than he followed her out. "I called Laurence on my way to the hospital and asked about possibly meeting together. He's agreed to go over what they used to do, but he would rather meet with us by himself so Britan doesn't have to spend any extra time on her feet."

"Okay, sounds like a plan. Do you want me there?"

"Since we're supposed to be in this together, it might help."

They were in this together? He made it sound like they were an actual team.

Well, they were, right?

Yes, but only a professional team. Which was what he'd meant, of course.

"Did he give you a time frame?"

"Tonight after work, since this needs to happen fairly quickly? That system is either going to dissipate or strengthen, so I don't want to wait too long."

Tonight after work. "I have Claire..."

He nodded. "I know. Would it upset her to hear us talk about this?"

"No, I don't think so, since it's still kind of nebulous. We could order takeout and then do it—where? In your office?"

Do it in his office? Why did everything she said seem to have some hidden meaning all of a sudden? She quickly corrected herself. "We could have the *meeting* in your office, I mean."

"I knew what you meant." That corner of his mouth popped up again. "Okay, I'll meet you there with dinner. Anything you don't like?"

"I like everything."

Ugh! Again? Seriously? This time, Seb's glance slid from her eyes to her lips and hung there for a second. She wasn't the only one who was taking things the wrong way, it would seem.

"I'll just take my best guess, then. Seven o'clock? Does that give you enough time to get Claire and bring her back here?"

"It does. I'll see you at seven, then."

With that, Sebastien finally headed in a direction that was different from her trajectory, and she was glad. Because she didn't know how much longer she could have pretended that everything was just fine.

When it really wasn't.

* * *

He hoped she liked fish.

Seb couldn't remember what Rachel had eaten at the restaurant a year ago. Because he'd been too busy trying not to notice how beautiful she was. And when she'd thrown her head back and laughed at something stupid he'd said, the long line of her neck stood out in sharp relief in the muted lighting of the restaurant. He wasn't even sure why he'd wound up at the restaurant that night, other than the fact that it was close to the hospital and he'd been hungry. He hadn't even cared when they'd asked if he would mind sharing his table.

Looking back, that had not been the smartest move.

Adjusting the takeout bags in his hands, he arrived back at his office in time to see Rachel and Claire get off the elevator. He'd tried to get a sampling of several things from the restaurant. Surely there'd be at least something that they would like.

He opened the door enough to motion them inside. Claire was a tall, lanky girl with hair as dark as her mom's.

He followed them in, and Rachel held up a couple of bags. "I brought plates and plastic cutlery."

"Good thinking." Unlike him, since the thought of plates hadn't even crossed his mind.

In fact, these days he didn't seem to think through much at all.

He'd briefly caught sight of Claire a time or two at the hospital but had never actually spoken to her before that day when he'd examined her. His eyes went to her neck, looking for any remaining swelling. If there was, it was no longer visible. A good sign.

He forced a smile. "How are you feeling?" He glanced at Rachel. "And it's Sebastien or Seb, remember?" He glanced over at Rachel to make sure she still didn't object.

"Sebastien is such a cool name."

"You think?"

Claire cocked her head. "Yep. It has a neat pronunciation."

Okay, well, that was the first time he'd ever heard that one. "Well, thank you very much." He held up the bags he had in both hands. "How about we serve this on the desk?"

"That looks like a ton of food."

He shrugged. "I wasn't sure what everyone liked. I'll go ahead and start setting it out."

Taking the containers out of the bag, he opened the largest one first, hearing an exclamation of surprise from behind him.

"*Poisson cru!* I love that."

He turned and found it was Claire who'd said it, not Rachel. His brows went up. "You've had *poisson cru* before?"

"Yes, someone brought it to school for a special birthday lunch one time. You had your choice of that or hot dogs." She made a face when she said that last word.

He couldn't blame her. Faced with that same choice, he was pretty sure which one he'd have elected to eat.

Stuffed inside coconut shells, the mixture of raw tuna, lime, coconut juice, tomatoes and cucumber was a national dish among the French Polynesian islands. "Do you know what the Tahitian word for it is?"

Claire frowned for a minute as she thought. "*Ota* something?"

"Close. It's *e'ia ota.*"

The girl pronounced the words carefully. "We're learning some Tahitian in school—and French—but Tahitian is really hard."

Seb had grown up learning it, since his mom was Tahitian. But he could see that it wasn't an easy language. "I think English is pretty difficult, too."

"But you speak it so well."

"We hear it a lot." He paused. "Tell you what. If you ever have any questions about Tahitian or French, you can ask me, okay?"

Rachel took a step forward, interrupting the exchange. "Well, I'm sure you have better things to do with your time. And with all of this delicious-smelling food sitting here, I'm starting to get hungry. Are we ready to eat?"

He guessed he'd been put in his place. It was pretty obvious that while Rachel might not mind her daughter using his first name, she did not want him involved in her life. And that was fine with him. In fact, it had provided the wake-up call he'd needed. In reality, he'd had no idea why he'd offered to help her learn Tahitian. It had been impulsive.

Like sleeping with her mother?

Exactly like that. The last thing he needed was to get attached to Rachel or her daughter.

She handed them each a plate and put some utensils in each of the food containers to serve it. She moved closer to him and lowered her voice. "I didn't mean what I said in a rude way. I just don't want her imposing on your time. I know you're busy."

He hadn't realized how tense he'd gotten until his muscles went slack. At least she didn't think he was some creep trying to push his way into their lives. That was the last thing he wanted to do.

What he'd vowed after Bleu's death still held.

He did not want to be a father. Not now. Not in the future.

He waited for Rachel and her daughter to help themselves to the offerings, glad that they seemed to like everything on the desk. He hadn't been too sure about getting the *e'ia ota*, but as strange as the dish sounded, most people who tried it liked it.

Claire sat on one of the office chairs near the food, while Seb and her mom went over to the small love seat, setting their plates on the coffee table. Rather than sit next to her, he chose one of the two chairs across from her, lowering himself into it. Rachel was looking down at her plate with a weird half smile on her face.

"What?" he asked.

"Nothing, really," she said. "It's kind of weird working together, isn't it?"

Was he that easy to read?

"A little. But it's not something we can't handle."

Claire's voice carried across. "This is really good. And how did you know mango was my favorite fruit?"

He allowed himself to smile. "Isn't it everyone's?"

"It should be."

The rest of the meal was spent in companionable silence, with Claire occasionally asking how to say different Tahitian words.

When they cleaned up the food, stowing the leftovers in his office fridge, Rachel stood. "Claire, can you do your homework while Seb and I get some work done?"

"Are you going to see patients?"

"No, we're just making sure the hospital's rules and regulations are up to date."

She sidestepped the real reason for this meeting. As much as she'd said it wouldn't bother Claire to know there was a low-pressure system hanging out somewhere in the ocean, Rachel evidently didn't want her sitting right next to them while they discussed it.

That was fine with him. The less he had to interact with the girl, the better. And honestly, despite her earlier words, Rachel probably felt the same way. One thing he definitely didn't want was for her to start looking at him as some sort of father figure, because that was a recipe for hurt feelings. He didn't know if Claire's biological dad was out of the picture or if she was the result of a sperm donor, and really, the less he knew about it, the easier it would be to keep himself from doing something stupid.

Like getting attached?

Exactly like that. He'd only been really attached to one child in his life. And that kid's name was inscribed on his shoulder.

Rachel lifted the lid to her laptop and started it up. Once it had, she opened a window that contained weather updates and the projected course for the low-pressure system. Another browser pane displayed hospital protocol. Laurence was supposed to have joined the meeting, but he'd had to cancel at the last minute due to dinner plans his wife had made without his knowledge. And since the other doctor really didn't want her to know he was going to meet with them, he couldn't just stop by.

"Okay, where do we start?"

"Let's start with the evacuation plans."

She scrolled down the different emergency protocols the hospital had in place. When she found cyclones, she stopped, and they both scanned the document that had been updated last year. The bullet points laid things out step by step, moving from the least urgent scenario to the worst.

Not too bad. "Okay, here's how evacuations work." She used her pen to point to an area on the screen.

There were four medical centers on the island, ranging from a community prevention clinic that was only staffed once a week to Taurati's largest facility, which was Centre Hospitalier.

"Oh, my," she murmured.

Since Hospitalier was the biggest, it also had the most responsibility, having to make sure all the medical facilities were locked down and gathering records for patients who were actively being treated. Everything from ingrown toenails to chemo patients would have to be listed and accounted for, both before and after a storm hit.

"Yes, I know." Seb had figured it was going to be a huge task, and he could also see why Laurence had wanted to hand it off this year. "Let's look at storm projections."

They popped open the other screen, and Rachel slowly scrolled so that they could both read. "Oh, no. It's just become more organized."

"I see that."

"What's become more organized?"

Seb and Rachel jerked their heads up to see that Claire was standing there with an open textbook in her hands.

Rachel's eyes widened even as Claire moved closer, trying to read what they were looking at.

"Is that a storm?" Claire's book closed with a snap. Her voice lowered to a whisper. "Is it going to hit Taurati?"

CHAPTER FIVE

"It's the beginnings of a storm, but no one knows where it's going yet or if it will get any stronger. Right now there's nothing to worry about." Rachel had said it was okay if Claire overheard them, but now she wasn't so sure. The *poisson cru* that had been so delicious a half hour earlier now sat in her stomach like a rock.

But her daughter had handled worse. Far worse than a storm that would probably blow itself out in a week.

"Then why are you looking at news articles about it? Is that the reason *you're* here?" The last question was aimed at Sebastien.

Sebastien gave her a smile. "You mean having dinner in my office isn't enough of a reason?"

Claire studied him for a minute. Her daughter was intuitive, maybe because of what she'd been through in her short life. Suddenly she smiled. "Well, it was pretty good."

Going over to give her a hug, Rachel said, "If the storm gets to be a problem, I'll be honest and tell you, okay? Grams has already called me, and she said she'll fly in to get you and take you back to the States if it looks like it's going to be a direct hit."

"But what about you?"

That was a harder question. Flying away before the hospital was officially under an evacuation order seemed horribly selfish. And the storm had just now been upgraded from a tropical disturbance to a tropical depression. "Honey, I have to stay. If they evacuate the hospital, I'll help with that, and then I'll join you. I just don't want to have to worry about you being at home alone while that's going on. We're all hoping the storm will just dissipate over the next couple of days."

What was the likelihood of that happening, when it seemed it was beginning to get more organized instead?

"And you'll tell me before you ask Grams to come get me?"

"I will. But for now you need to let us work, and you probably have more homework to do, do you not?"

"Yes, but—"

"But nothing. Homework."

Claire gave a dramatic sigh and then headed back to the desk with her schoolbook.

The next two hours were spent reviewing what the hospital already had in place and trying to find any holes in the plans. But it didn't look like there were any. The most critical patients would be airlifted to places outside the storm radius, while those who were less serious would be given the option of going to stay with family on the island or elsewhere. A skeleton crew would remain at the hospital to deal with the aftermath of the storm and to help any injured residents.

"Looks like Laurence and Britan—and those who worked on it before they took it over—have done a great job with things," said Sebastien. "According to this, we'll need to notify staff when the island is officially in the storm's path and is upgraded to a severe tropical storm. Although by then most people on the island will be following the weather reports. I'm sure most residents will remember Tropical Cyclone Wasa-Arthur and will start preparing. We'll want to take care of any…travel arrangements before that time."

She appreciated him speaking in low tones and using ambiguous terms. Although when she glanced up, Rachel seemed to be buried in her studies, her head down, writing furiously on a pad of paper.

"Since Wisconsin isn't actually a hub of hurricanes, you'll have to keep me apprised of the different kinds of classifications."

"They're similar to hurricane classifications as far as wind speed. They just use different terminology."

"How many patients do we have right now?"

"Fortunately, we don't have the numbers that we did a couple of years ago, so I'd say we're not quite at half capacity right now. But if people start doing stupid things while preparing for the storm, we could see an uptick in injuries from power tools and the like."

"Ugh." Power-tool injuries could run the gamut from minor annoyances to life-threatening injuries. She'd seen more than her share of severed fingers from table saws. "Those are never fun."

"No." He glanced down at the paperwork. "Looks like if we get bumped up to a tropical low, then we'll start handing out flyers on storm preparedness, which has a section on tool safety and emergency first aid in case of accidents."

"How much of an uptick in patients could we see?"

He shrugged. "This will be my first major

storm here. I'm sure there are statistics somewhere, though."

"Okay. We'll need to ask departments to take
stock of their inventory so we can see if we can
get in what is needed before we're too far along
in the process."

"I was thinking the same thing."

She glanced at Claire again, but she still
looked immersed in her studies. Wait. Her
books were open, but her pencil was now down,
and she had her phone out. "Claire? What are
you doing?"

"Texting some of my friends to see if they've
heard the news."

Her heart dropped. "Don't do that! Not yet!"
She got control of her voice, but it took some
doing. "How many have you texted?"

"Just my best friend. She said she hasn't
heard anything."

Rachel's eyes closed for a second as frus-
tration pulsed through her. That was all they
needed—for her daughter to start a mass panic.

As if guessing her thoughts, Seb slid his hand
over hers. "It's okay," he murmured. "People
will have already heard about the storm."

The gravel of his voice and warmth of his
skin sent a shiver over her, and she realized
she'd been holding herself as rigid as a piece
of iron pipe.

"I'm sorry, Mom."

"It's my fault. I should have asked you not to text anyone yet. But Sebastien is right. People have undoubtedly already heard. But let's let parents inform their kids in their own timing, okay?"

"Okay. If someone texts me about it, am I allowed to say anything?"

"Not about our work here, because we're dealing with worst-case scenarios, and we don't want to scare anyone unnecessarily. But you can certainly talk with your friends using generalities."

"Generalities. Like if I'm nervous and stuff like that?"

"Yes. Exactly like that."

Sebastien let go of her hand, and she realized how calming his presence was. If only he'd been there when Claire was going through treatments. She could have used his steady confidence. But he hadn't been. And she'd proved to herself that she really didn't need anyone. Despite that crazy night they'd spent together a year earlier, she didn't need him, either, right? Didn't want him intruding into her space with Claire. Not when they were just getting island living down to a science and figuring out how to do things without having the safety net of her parents or childhood friends nearby.

And the thought of having Sebastien as a safety net? It was terrifying. And impossible. His attempt at deflecting her fear about the storm had worked far too well. Claire had no experience with men other than knowing her father had abandoned her. But unlike Rachel, her daughter wasn't hardened or cynical, so it would be too easy for someone to hurt her without even realizing they'd done it. Not that Rachel believed the pediatrician would purposely try to hurt Claire. But she didn't want to take the chance of her getting attached and then being devastated when Seb slipped off her radar without a word.

So from here on out, she was going to be careful how much contact she allowed them to have with each other. Even if it meant shipping Claire off with her mom earlier than she'd planned. She'd call Wisconsin tonight and ask her mother to check flights to Tahiti for the next couple of days so, if possible, she'd be prepared to pick Claire up and take her home.

Then she could work with Sebastien without worrying that she would be putting her daughter's heart in danger.

Or hers?

No, hers wasn't in danger. If the night they'd spent together hadn't left a mark, then she should be safe.

At least that was her hope. And if she was wrong?

Then she would have to find a way to interact with him as little as possible. Or she'd have to make a choice she didn't want to make.

The pamphlets were printed up a day later, and his plan was to distribute them to each department in the hospital. Seb almost passed them out himself but realized leaving Rachel out of the process wasn't right or fair. Instead, he contacted her to let her know what he'd done and asked her to swing by the office.

Eating with her and Claire in his office had given him an odd warmth in his chest that had set off alarm bells, and when her daughter had been afraid, it had seemed far too natural for Seb to make a quip about dinner to allay her fears. Just as he'd done in the exam room. He'd never hesitated or remained silent to let Rachel deal with it in her own way. No, he'd jumped right in. The way a father might have?

Hell, he hoped not. But deep down, he wondered. He could argue it away by saying he was just doing what any friend of the family might have done, but he wasn't Rachel's friend, despite having been her lover for a night.

A knock sounded at the door of his office as

he was reviewing a patient's chart, and he immediately tensed.

"Come in."

The door opened and closed with a quiet click before he looked up from his computer. He knew who it was even before his eyes came up to meet hers.

She came over to his desk, and before he could say anything, she picked up a brochure and looked at it.

"Everything okay?" he asked.

"Not really."

Something spiked through his chest. "Claire?"

"No. You. What are these?" She held up one.

He frowned. "Our pamphlets. They're what I texted you about."

"I thought we were supposed to be working together on these. But it looks like you went on without me." Her voice was very soft. A warning sign if he'd ever heard one.

She studied one of the pamphlets that had the phrase *l'avertissement* printed in bold type across the front. The bulk of it contained all the things they had talked about yesterday.

"I thought we did work on this together."

"Really?" Her brows went up. "I don't remember helping to print these up."

"You're right. I probably shouldn't have. I remember you telling Neves that you needed to limit your time to when you're here at the hospital. I don't have anyone at home who… needs me."

Merde. That had come out sounding pretty pathetic. But it was true.

Her face softened, and her brow cleared. "Sorry, you're right, and they look great. I just don't want you to feel you have to carry this on your own. Just because I have a child and you don't, that doesn't mean I can't carry an equal amount of the work."

Those words cut through his gut like a knife.

Just because I have a child and you don't…

She had no idea that he'd give anything to be in the position she was. Where he had to worry about his *fils* being scared because of an oncoming storm. Or have to distract him with humor or divert him by telling him to do his homework.

If only Rachel knew how very fortunate she was.

Except he was pretty sure she did know.

He opened his mouth to correct her about his not having a child before closing it again. Wasn't this the reason his hair was so long? Why he was avoiding going to get it cut or trying not to talk about having a child who'd passed away?

He didn't need her pity or her sympathy. And

that hadn't been what this conversation was about. It was about the division of labor. She was irritated that he'd taken it upon himself to do something without consulting her.

And she was right.

"I'm sorry, Rachel. I should have waited to print them off until you had a chance to review them. Thanks for calling me out on it."

She came in and sat in one of the chairs in front of his desk. "I wasn't trying to call you out on it. Not really. Is this why you wanted to see me?"

"Yes. Why don't you take one and look through it?"

"I trust you. Besides—" One corner of her mouth quirked. "Claire tells me my French needs some work, so I'd be no good at giving you an honest opinion on that."

"I've heard you speak a couple of times. It's not that bad."

Rachel groaned. "That's not much of an endorsement." She drew a deep breath. "I do need to talk to you about something besides the pamphlet, though."

"Oh?"

She hesitated before saying, "I called my mom yesterday evening after I got home and asked her to check on flights. Just in case this thing blows up more quickly than we expect it to."

"That doesn't surprise me. We talked about the possibility of Claire going back to the States."

"Yes…well, my mom called this morning and said she'd found a flight that was incredibly low and went ahead and booked it. Without asking me first."

"Ah…" He could definitely see why coming to his office and finding the pamphlets already printed up could have *énervé* her, making her feel like everyone was sidestepping her wishes. "And here I am doing something without asking you first. Again, I'm sorry. Truly."

"It's okay. I'm just edgy with everything happening so fast."

"I can understand that." His head tilted. "When is your mom arriving?"

"Tomorrow morning."

"Wow, that *was* fast." He sighed. "But maybe it's for the best. There has been a marginal increase in the storm's intensity."

"I know. I saw it." Her hands twined together in her lap. "And I do want Claire out of the equation, if possible. But Mom hasn't booked their flight home yet, so she's going to stay with Claire for a couple of days and see how things go. If it dissipates, she'll have had a nice visit with her granddaughter."

"That sounds like a good plan."

She then smiled. "And then you won't have to worry about waking me in the middle of the night when you need something."

Like he had in that cabana the night they were together? That whole experience had been surreal and so not like him. But she'd been soft and warm and oh, so sexy with her hair tumbled across those pillows. He'd gotten up to leave in the middle of the night and then found he couldn't. So he'd climbed back in bed and woken her. And when those deep brown eyes opened…

He realized she'd asked him something and blinked back to the present. "Sorry, I missed that."

"I just wanted to know if there was any increase in injuries, since I did see suggestions online for fortifying housing structures in case the storm does hit the island."

"No, not yet. But it won't be long. Is Claire in school today?"

"Yes. I told her teacher that she may be visiting her grandmother in Wisconsin, just so they'd be aware. They're going to get some lessons together, just in case. No one seemed overly alarmed. Yet."

No, that would come later. It was one thing being hit by a hurricane in a big country like the United States, when you could truly evacuate and leave for an unaffected area. On an island like Taurati, however, there were only so many options. If you were lucky enough to have relatives somewhere else, you could leave. If your whole life was on this island, sometimes your only option was to hunker down and pray for the best.

"Let's hope there's not any reason to be alarmed and that Claire simply gets some quality time with her grandmother."

"I truly hope that's how things go."

He glanced at her. "When will you leave?"

"I won't go until we get what we need done at the hospital."

He wasn't sure he liked that idea, and he wasn't sure why. "And if it's too late to evacuate by that time?"

She shrugged. "I can't think that far ahead."

"You may have to. You do have a daughter to think of."

"I know. But I can't just leave my patients or leave the hospital shorthanded. Not yet."

The intercom came on. "Trauma team to the ER. Trauma team to the ER."

Seb winced. "When did you say you saw that internet article?"

"This morning." Her lips twisted. "Surely not."

"You never know. I'm going down there to see if I can lend a hand."

"Me, too. Do you want me to wait for you?"

Seb stood. "I'm ready now. So let's go."

Once they got to the ground floor, a chaotic scene met their eyes. There were several ambulances in the bay and blood pooling on the ground from someone on a nearby stretcher—several layers of bandaging wrapped around his head. Seb found the nearest EMT. "What do we have?"

"Some friends were trying to cut down a tree they said was too close to the house because of the threat of a cyclone. A chain saw, some ropes and large swinging branches did not make for a happy scene. We have some broken bones, and a dropped chain saw hit one man in the head. He's alive, but…"

Merde. His eyes met Rachel's, and he gave a quick nod before jumping into the fray and helping the nearest patient.

It had started.

Rachel found herself helping stabilize an open tibial fracture in one of the surgical suites. A teenaged girl had held her arm up to ward off the huge tree limb that had careened her way. The maneuver had worked, the branch missing her head, but instead it had snapped her arm in two with enough force to drive the bone through the skin.

The girl was a little older than Claire, and it sent a pang of fear through her. Who ever thought that something so terrible could happen to their child? She answered her own question. No one ever expected the worst to happen to them. They expected their lives to run according to a certain plan.

Hadn't she been the same? She'd never dreamed Claire's father would leave them. Or that Claire would get cancer a few years later.

There were no promises. No guarantees in life. It was one reason she didn't date. Hadn't since Claire's diagnosis. In fact, one of the only two sexual encounters she'd had since then had been with Sebastien. And that hadn't gone according to plan, either. She'd expected a quick hour or two that she could dust from her hands afterward.

Instead it had been…

Complicated.

The doctor treating the girl had lavaged the area to clean it before asking Rachel to maintain steady traction on the fracture so they could maneuver the bone back into place. This was the third try. Monica was fortunately sedated, but the process still made Rachel cringe.

There was no help for it, though. Rachel closed her eyes for a second to block the out the sight of the streaky tears that were still visible on the child's face. She'd been in agony during the ride over and during the triage process in the ER.

But what Rachel couldn't block out were her thoughts. Monica's dad was still being treated for a head injury, and her brother had a broken clavicle. So much heartache in one family. The mother was stationed in the waiting room, beside herself, as each member of her immediate family had been wheeled in separate directions to be treated.

Rachel was pretty sure Monica's brother would be okay. But her dad? All they could do was their best.

The ortho's voice brought her back. "Okay, I think we got it. Go ahead and gradually release the pressure and see if it stays in place." They would flush the site again as soon as it was stabilized and X-ray it to make sure it was stable before casting her forearm.

They held their breath as Rachel gingerly reduced the traction. Okay. There was no popping sensation of a bone slipping out of place.

"Good. Let's get that X-ray and pray the blood supply to the bone wasn't compromised."

If that happened, that portion of the bone would die and the fracture would not heal.

They'd have to go back in and take out the dead section, grafting healthy bone onto the end.

The X-ray showed—just as the orthopedist thought—that the ends of the bone were lined up and so far holding.

"I'm going to flush it out again, and we'll put a temporary cast in place until tomorrow. I want one last X-ray before we do anything permanent. I'm hoping we can get by without pins."

Rachel wasn't a surgical nurse, but because each of the three operating bays was needed for injured patients, she'd had to fill in, which she'd gladly done. She wondered which patient Seb had. The scene had been so chaotic, she'd lost track of him almost as soon as they'd come onto the floor. And then she'd been whisked into surgery along with her current patient.

Fortunately—if there was such a thing for a situation like this—the accident had occurred during daylight hours, when there was more than just a skeleton crew on duty.

The flushing of Monica's arm was quick but thorough, and some medication to manage pain was administered through her IV before the wound was closed and they woke her up.

A tense minute or two went by as the girl lay motionless on the table. Then her head turned from side to side, and her eyes fluttered open.

The surgeon leaned over the table. "Monica, can you hear me?"

She slowly nodded her head, gaze tracking to her doctor's face. Rachel hadn't realized how rock-hard her muscles had gone until that moment. But she relaxed all at once, wiggling her shoulders to throw off the last of the tension.

The cell phone in her pocket buzzed, but she ignored it, hoping it wasn't Claire with an emergency of her own. Their signal for that was for Claire to call back immediately after the first attempt.

She waited with bated breath, but the phone remained still. Once the patient went to recovery, she'd give a quick glance at the readout before heading back to the ER to see if there was anything else she could help with.

And to see if she could spot Seb?

No. Of course not. She was in the ER because she was needed. Not because of him.

"Okay, it looks like your arm is going to be fine," the surgeon was telling Monica. "We'll probably keep you overnight so we can put some antibiotics through your IV line. And then tomorrow we'll get you casted up and on your way."

Monica's pupils were still pretty unfocused, but she seemed to understand what the doctor was saying, because she nodded again.

The surgeon glanced around the space. "Thank you. Good work."

Rachel nodded and started pulling off her mask and gloves to prepare to leave. She needed to get in contact with her mom and get more details on her flight and how this was all going to work. Her mom was scheduled to land in Tahiti, which had an international airport, then finish the trip to Taurati on a smaller plane, which she hadn't booked yet. And once news of the growing storm hit, flights in and out would be harder to come by.

If Rachel wasn't required in the ER, she'd take a break and see if she could find a flight in and out of the smaller island. And she needed to break the news to Claire.

The surgeon smiled at her. "I haven't seen you in surgery before."

She'd never really spoken with Dr. Chauvre before, and even though the hospital wasn't huge by most standards, they still kind of kept to their departments and just saw other hospital staff in passing. "That's because I'm not a surgical nurse. I work in Pediatrics. They just needed some extra hands."

"Well, I was impressed. Any chance we can lure you over to the dark side… I mean Ortho?" His grin revealed straight white teeth and a dimple in his right cheek. "I'm serious. I'm not just saying it."

Well, that was a first. She'd never had a doctor try to talk her into changing departments before. She didn't know quite what to say, but she was flattered. If she did move, she would see Seb about as often as she'd seen Dr. Chauvre—just in passing and not very often. Hadn't she thought about how much easier that would be?

But she loved pediatrics. Had shifted over to it after Claire was diagnosed and treated.

She forced a smile. "How dark could it be, really? Let me think about it. I'm not sure the hospital would even let me transfer over."

"Oh, they would." Another smile.

Okay, that was weird. Did he have some pull with the administration?

"Well, that's good to know. I'll think about it and let you know if it's something I want to pursue."

"That's all I can ask." He glanced at the door. "On to the next patient. If you're interested, come up to the fourth floor and we can talk."

"I will. Thanks again."

She ducked out of the room, her face warm with the flush of pleasure. Good to know that someone wanted her.

Not that Pediatrics didn't. It had just been

weird over the last couple of days having to work with Sebastien. It wasn't his fault that the hospital administrator had tossed them into the ring together. He had no idea what had transpired between the two of them.

Although Seb seemed much less bothered about it than she did. Or maybe he was equally good at hiding it.

Maybe he would even be happier if she were no longer in Pediatrics. The thought made her deflate a little. Perhaps that's why Dr. Chauvre's offer was so attractive. Because Sebastien didn't seem to quake each time he looked at her?

Things were such a mess. She'd sworn she wasn't getting involved with another man until Claire was grown-up and gone. She wanted her daughter to be able to enjoy her childhood without the stress of trying to find where she fit in the picture with any relationship Rachel might have. Why did the six years until Claire's eighteenth birthday suddenly seem so far away?

Damn. She needed to just enjoy her daughter while she was still at home. And if she let herself fret over Sebastien Deslaurier each and every day, she was not going to be able to do that. But she wasn't going to think about moving. Not until the current crisis with the storm was over and gone. Then she was really going to have to give some thought to how she wanted to spend the rest of her time on the island. However long that might be.

CHAPTER SIX

"What is Dr. Chauvre's first name?"

"What?" Rachel's reappearance in the ER surprised Seb. He'd assumed she'd gone back to Pediatrics after whatever patient she'd been helping with.

He'd finished treating the boy with the broken leg and had helped stabilize the kid's father, who'd been struck with the chain saw. It had been touch and go since the blade had glanced off the man's head with enough force to breach the skull. It looked like the brain itself had been spared, although there was always the possibility of swelling from trauma. The patient wasn't out of the woods yet.

She wouldn't quite meet his eyes. "I was just in surgery with him and realized I didn't know his full name."

"It's Philippe." That was odd. Although Sebastien had been at the hospital long enough to know most of the staff members by name—

first and last—it just seemed an out-of-the-blue question. As was the fact that she was still not quite holding his glance. "How did surgery go?"

"It went well. We were able to get Monica's arm back in place, and she's awake. The arm has a temporary cast that will be replaced tomorrow if everything looks stable."

"Good news."

"How about the other victims? Are they doing okay?"

"Yes," he said. "Even the head injury patient is stable for the moment. All in all, that family was very lucky."

"Yes." This time she did meet his eyes. "It's funny how we classify luck sometimes, isn't it?"

He hadn't thought about it much, but she was probably right. Hadn't he thought about the fact that even though Claire had had cancer that Rachel was lucky enough to still have her?

Rachel probably thought the same thing about someone whose child came through with some minor illness or injury: well, at least they didn't have to deal with cancer.

"Yes, it is." He paused before deciding to change the subject. "Any word on your mom's arrival?"

"Oh, damn. My phone rang while I was in

surgery, then Dr. Chauvre wanted to speak with me afterward and I completely forgot."

He'd wanted to speak to her afterward?

Rachel fished her phone out of her pocket and glanced at the readout. "It's Claire."

Without saying anything else, she pressed a button on her phone, mouthing *sorry* at him.

He wasn't sure whether he should just walk away and give her some privacy or if she wanted to touch base about the storm.

"Hi, honey. Are you okay?"

He watched her body language, glad when she drew a deep breath and blew it out. "She did? What time does she arrive on the island?"

Claire must have said something else, because Rachel listened without speaking for a minute or two. "Like I told you yesterday, it was Grams's idea. I didn't call her and ask her to pick you up this soon. And no, the storm isn't dangerous at the moment. It might never be. But since she's coming, I don't think it's a bad idea to go back to her house for a short vacation if the storm gets worse. She's missed you."

Rachel's eyes suddenly jerked to his. "I—I'm not sure what Sebastien's schedule is, sweetie."

His schedule? Why would she want to know his schedule?

Whatever Claire said next made her mom

suck down a quick breath. "I'll ask him. But no promises."

"Ask me what?"

There was a deer-in-the-headlights moment before she put her hand over the bottom of the phone. "She wants to come by the hospital tomorrow with my mom to see you, since she doesn't know when she'll need to leave the island."

She did? He wasn't sure why she wanted to do that, but it made something burn in his chest. "Of course she can. Just let me know what time, and as long as there's not an emergency I need to deal with, I'll be happy to see her."

Rachel gave him a slight smile and mouthed *thank you.* "He said he'll try. We'll work out the time with Grams tonight, okay? I'll bring some food home with me." There was a pause. "I'm sure he has other things to do tonight. See you when I get there. Let Grams know what the plan is for dinner."

She hung up the phone. "Sorry. I thought it was an emergency or I wouldn't have subjected you to that."

Subjected him to what? Her end of the conversation? Or Claire wanting to stop by? So if he hadn't been standing there, he probably never would have known.

It didn't matter. He wasn't sure why he'd been so quick to agree to Claire stopping by to see him, other than the fact that he didn't want to have any regrets if the storm wreaked havoc and Claire and Rachel left the island, and he never saw them again.

The burning in his chest grew at that thought.

It was also obvious that Claire had wanted to invite him over to their apartment for a meal, and Rachel had been quick to put the kibosh on that. As well she should have. Intruding in that space where Rachel, Claire and her mom would try to talk while none of them admitted how scared they were about that situation that hovered a thousand miles offshore put a lump in his throat. How did you leave things when you weren't sure if it was the last time you were ever going to see each other?

Maybe that was part of the reason why Layla's parents kept sending him Christmas cards—there'd never been any true goodbyes said. Layla had left without ever saying she wasn't coming back to the house. And he'd never gotten in contact with her. Instead, their unfinished business hovered out there in the ether, kind of like that storm offshore.

It might be time to pick up a pen and write Layla and her parents a letter, finally cutting the last of those ties and wishing them well.

Bleu really was the only thing that connected them now, and that thread was frayed so deeply that one hard tug and it would be over.

"You're fine, Rach. Nothing to apologize for."

She blinked, then stared down at her feet for a second. "I...um, appreciate that. And if you decide you'd rather not meet with Claire, I'll certainly understand. Please don't feel pressured to do anything you don't want to do."

"I do want to. I know what it feels like to not have closure."

Her head cocked to the side for a second before she sighed and nodded. "Yeah. So do I. What time do you work tomorrow, so I can kind of coordinate times?"

"I'm scheduled at eight and will be here the whole day, so whenever they arrive will be fine."

"Perfect."

It wasn't. But he wasn't going to tell her that. He was just going to show up and start doing what he hadn't done for years—close chapters so they weren't left hanging open in his life. Doing that with Claire and Rachel might be a great place to start. Despite the fact that that chapter had barely been opened.

Seb's phone buzzed, and he glanced down

at the readout before swearing softly, tapping something on his screen.

"What is it?"

He moved closer, holding his phone so they could both read the warning that was scrolling down his screen, before he realized she wouldn't be able to read the French fast enough to understand.

"The storm has strengthened far ahead of the predictions. So we'll need to get our evacuation plans underway."

"How far away is it?"

"It's still moving in this direction, although its trajectory has changed a bit, canting more to the north. But it's still uncertain where it might make landfall first. Although somewhere in the Leeward Islands is the best guess."

That might be good news for Taurati but would be very bad for some of the islands to their west.

Her hair grazed his chin as she tilted her head to try to look at the small image on his phone, and a mixture of coconut and vanilla hit his senses. He swallowed, forcing his glance to stay on his phone.

"What do we need to do?"

He tried to think past the sense of awareness that was now swinging through him. "I know you said you were going to take food home to

Claire and your mom. But is there any chance they could come here instead? I think we may have to work through the night, just in case. Or if you can't—"

"My mom can watch Claire, so I can. And I will. Let me go call her."

"Tell her she may need to take Claire back to the States sooner rather than later."

She bit her lip and stepped away. "Okay."

Rachel waited for her mom and Claire to arrive at the hospital. She was nervous, and she wasn't sure why. She really didn't want her mom meeting Sebastien, although she couldn't put a finger on why that was. Maybe it was the stress over the storm. Maybe it was because she felt the less Seb knew about her the better, especially since Claire had seemed far too interested in keeping in touch with him. But how could she try to discourage Claire when Sebastien had been the one to calm her daughter's nerves both when she was sick and when she realized there was a storm that would possibly head in Taurati's direction?

Rachel wasn't used to anyone helping with her daughter other than her parents. It had felt good to be able to sit back and let someone else reassure her. Too good, in fact.

It would be all too easy to get used to that.

But she had to remember that eventually he wasn't going to be in their lives, so she had to be careful about letting her daughter think that he was anything permanent. He was a work colleague, and that was it. That was all it would ever be.

Sebastien arrived before her mom and Claire did, lugging two bags of food from a local take-out joint.

"Wow, that looks like enough to feed an army."

"It's not. I just decided to get some typical American-style food. Fried chicken."

That made her smile. "Claire will love that. Thank you."

"There was no *salade de pomme de terre*—er…you call it potato salad? They were sold out."

"That's okay. It's not her favorite anyway. And she loves Taurati's food."

He pulled out a mango. "Especially this?"

"Yes. Especially that."

Just then she heard a familiar voice coming from the elevator, which had just arrived on their floor.

Claire appeared first and came careening toward her, arms outstretched. She gave her a big hug. "Grams says we have to leave tomorrow and that you're not coming. Why?"

Her mom, making her way toward them, gave a half shrug. "I didn't think it was my place to tell her without you there."

"It's okay. She knows what's happening for the most part."

Rachel watched as Sebastien smiled at Claire's greeting. Unlike Dr. Chauvre and his perfectly straight teeth, Seb's left canine stood at just a bit of an angle. That slight imperfection made him unique and added to his appeal rather than detracted from it. It was hard not to stare at his mouth every time he smiled. Made her want to do something to make those firm lips curve upward for that very reason.

Oh, girl, you are getting in too deep for your own good.

Realizing she actually had been staring at him, she cleared her throat to say something, but before she could, he nodded at the woman to her left. "This must be your mom?"

Great. Not only had she been staring, she'd evidently forgotten her manners as well. Something about this man made her normally orderly thoughts turn topsy-turvy. "I'm sorry. Yes, this is Marion Palmer. Mom, this is Dr. Deslaurier. I've been working with him on storm preparedness for the hospital."

"So you told me on the phone." Her mom held out her hand, eyes fixed on Seb's face.

"Nice to meet you. I trust you'll make her leave the island, if it comes down to it."

"Mom!" Her voice was a little sharper than she'd meant it to be, and she sent her mom a wordless apology before adding, "I will follow the recommendations of the island's officials and hospital administration."

If Sebastien was shocked at her mom's demand, he didn't show it. "Your daughter has a good head on her shoulders. I trust her to do the right thing."

Did he? Did that mean if she decided to move to Orthopedics, he would support her in that decision? Not something she wanted to think about right now.

Claire turned back to face her. "So why are we leaving, anyway?"

"The storm is bigger and moving faster than it was before." She tried to choose her words carefully. "It looks like it might hit one of the smaller islands west of here, and if that happens, there is going to be a lot of panic and maybe even some injuries. Part of my job is to help our patients here at Hospitalier, and I don't want to have to worry about you and whether or not you'll be okay."

"But what about that other island? The one that might be hit." She paused, head tilted as she evidently processed what Rachel had told her. "You're going to help them, too, right?"

"We're not positive yet that it's going to stay on the same path. It's changed a couple of times already."

"So it might not hit any of the islands?"

That was unlikely at this point. The islands of French Polynesia were scattered in a loose pattern, as if someone had skipped them across the ocean and left them where they landed. It would be hard for the tropical cyclone to miss all of them. The question was, would it hit the populated or unpopulated ones before continuing on its way? Their only hope was that the storm would weaken once it made landfall and pose less danger to the rest of the group.

She tried to figure out a way to explain their predicament. "They think it will hit at least some of them. We just don't know enough to say which ones yet. The bad news is, I have to work all night tonight, Claire, to make sure Hospitalier's patients have a place to go in case it does hit here first."

"I understand." Her daughter glanced at Sebastien. "You guys will be together the whole time, right?"

"What?"

"I'm scared you're going to be trapped somewhere by yourself and that…" Claire's eyes watered, and her voice trailed away.

"Hey, I'll make sure your mom is safe." The deep gruff tones from beside her made Rachel swallow, a shiver washing over her.

How long had it been since she'd had someone say something like that? She was normally the one having to make sure others were safe, because her experience was that no one else was going to do it for you. Roy had left her to do everything on her own, and when the going got really tough and he realized having a child would change his life, he'd literally left her to do it on her own. Rachel had sworn to herself that she *could* do it all.

But, man, it felt good to have someone stand there and imply that—if not outright say—she wasn't alone. Just like the other times that Seb had offered reassurance. God. Claire was worried that she might be trapped somewhere alone? Well, she needed to make sure she was ready to rescue herself rather than expect someone else to do it for her. Even if it was just emotionally.

It took another swallow and a few beats before Rachel could say anything at all. To hide her emotions, she enfolded her daughter in a tight hug. "Everyone at Hospitalier will be talking. We'll all be taking care of each other. So try not to worry, okay?"

She wasn't trying to discount Seb's offer to make sure she was okay, but, for Claire's sake, she had to be careful not to buy into that line of thinking, otherwise it would be that much harder when the extra support was withdrawn. And she was under no illusions about its permanence. Her ex had more than taught her that.

When she dared a quick glance beside her, she saw that Sebastien was frowning. But he didn't contradict her. Instead he said, "Well, we'd better eat before we have to get back to work."

"Can we eat on the beach?" Claire pulled her head from her mom's shoulder. "I haven't been able to go in a while."

Seb's frown eased. "I was thinking that exact thing. I even have a blanket in my closet that we can bring to sit on."

That might even be better. The ocean breeze might help to clear her head. Or at least it would prepare her for the reality that was to come.

Rachel took one of the bags of food and Claire the other while Seb got the blanket. She did her best to not to think about how this was the second time they would be sharing a meal together. Almost like a real...

No. They were not a family.

Leaving the hospital, they walked down the same boardwalk as the one where they'd helped to save Sharon's life. The lifeguard stand was empty, but that made sense, since it was getting to be late afternoon. Looking at the sky, you would still never know that a big storm was threatening to disrupt the idyllic life around them. Her mom glanced at her. "This is absolutely beautiful."

"You've been here before."

"Yes, but it's been a while, and I'd forgotten how lovely it is here."

Yes, it was. And Rachel made an effort not to take it—not to take *life*—for granted. She draped an arm across Claire's shoulder as they stepped onto the sand. "We really love it here, don't we, kiddo?"

"Yes, we do. I wish you and Gramps could come live with us."

Her mom laughed. "You will never get Gramps to leave Wisconsin."

It was the truth. Her dad had been raised on the farm where they currently lived. It wasn't very likely they would talk him into leaving it. And somehow, she couldn't see her dad in swim trunks hanging out on the beach. It just wasn't his style.

She glanced at Seb. "Where do you want to eat?"

"Let's go down a little farther. Maybe between here and the overwater cabanas."

She was glad he hadn't suggested eating inside one of them. Not only would it be warm this time of day, but she didn't want her mind to wander to another—more luxurious—cabana, where some pretty sexy things had happened. Especially not with Claire and her mom here.

They got to the spot, and Sebastien tossed out the blanket. It was larger than she'd expected, with plenty of room for them to spread out to eat.

"Ooh," said Claire as she took her plate. "I haven't had fried chicken since we left Wisconsin."

Rachel smiled at Seb. "Evidently that was a good choice."

While they ate, Seb regaled them with stories about things from his childhood. Claire sat there as if entranced by every word that came out of his mouth.

Rachel felt the same way. She knew he'd grown up in Tahiti, but she didn't realize he'd been a daredevil as a child. He seemed so… calm and unflappable nowadays. Maybe from the result of having a normal, happy childhood.

But then she remembered those whispers she'd overheard about something bad. From his childhood? Or from his later years?

He hadn't actually said anything about his teenaged or young adult years. Was that on purpose? Or was it just an oversight?

A slight movement from the waterline caught her attention, and she tensed. "Something's out there."

"Where?"

"To the right. About twenty or thirty yards." She stared at the spot, thinking maybe someone was swimming in the shallows, although the sun had all but disappeared from the horizon. She hadn't realized it had gotten so late. And then something slowly emerged from the water. And it wasn't a swimmer. Not a human one, anyway.

Seb squinted at the area she indicated and saw it in the shadows. A low shape, pulling itself forward with flippers. It was a sea turtle. He got the group's attention before putting his finger to his lips and making a low sound.

This was nesting season. They sat in silence on the warm sand so they didn't disturb the magnificent creature as she followed the instincts of her ancient ancestors and moved slowly, push by push, over the beach.

It was the first time Seb had actually witnessed this. He made a mental note to mark the spot once she was done so that one of the island's conservation groups could flag it. He wasn't sure what would—or even could—be done if Tropical Cyclone Koji actually made landfall on Taurati. But hopefully with the course being recalculated hourly, this nest would be spared.

Bit by bit, the turtle moved across the sand. There was an intimacy to the scene that was both sacred and profound. And it was hard not to feel a connection with the people he was with as they also watched the creature's progress. Then she passed them, continuing for a few yards before stopping. She looked neither right nor left. The nearby humans might not have even existed, for all the attention she paid them. Which was a good thing.

She stayed where she was for several minutes. Resting?

But then she started moving again, flippers pushing sand with an efficiency that was surprising in a creature that rarely ventured onto land. She was digging. Sebastien didn't dare move for fear of disturbing the turtle.

After what seemed like forever, she stopped again, and although he couldn't see from this distance, he was pretty sure she was busy laying her eggs.

No one said a word, and if he'd never seen this before, he was pretty sure this small group from Wisconsin had also never watched a sea turtle lay her eggs. Claire laid her head on her mom's shoulder, and Rachel grabbed her mom's hand.

A ribbon thread of jealousy went through him. Not for romantic reasons, but more a feeling of missing out on something important. Something he hadn't realized he'd lacked.

Thoughts of storms and loss were nowhere on his radar right now as the turtle showed them that special things only came with much effort.

Like having a family? Something he'd sworn he would never have again?

No, don't think about that right now. Not when you're tired and facing a situation that could prove to be life-threatening.

But the turtle didn't seem to care about any of those things. Didn't care that there might be a storm. Didn't care that her eggs might or might not make it. She could only do the things she had control over, and that was to find the safest environment she could for her eggs. And the stuff she couldn't control?

Well, that she left up to the universe.

Was that same universe trying to tell him something?

He had no idea. What he did know was that

he wasn't a turtle. He couldn't just act on sheer instinct and let the chips fall where they may.

But maybe none of that needed deciding right now. He could think about the lessons of this particular turtle later. But right now, couldn't he just live vicariously through Rachel's little family?

As if guessing his thoughts, a voice whispered into his ear, "She's so beautiful."

Rachel was right. And not just about the sea turtle. He found himself leaning closer, having to hold himself back from touching her. "Yes, she is, Rach."

She stared at him for a minute before giving him a smile that went straight to his head, even as a rock settled in his stomach. It would be so easy to give in to the fantasy that he belonged here. That that incredible smile had meant something special, and that this family was actually his.

For twenty minutes, time seemed to stand still. And for once he was okay with not hurrying it along.

Then the turtle's flippers started moving sand again. Only this time, she wasn't digging. Instead, she was pulling it over the top of her eggs. Little by little. Push by push. And when she was finished, she slowly trudged back across the beach, each pull seeming to take a

Herculean effort. But it was evidently worth it to her.

Something tickled at the back of his mind before he pushed it away again. He forced his attention back to the turtle.

She reached the surf, and a few more pushes had her buoyed up by the water. She soon disappeared from sight.

Trying not to disturb the group, he pulled his phone from his pocket and took a couple of pictures of the spot, using landmarks of the area to help conservationists find it.

"I can't believe we just witnessed that." Rachel's words were still low, even though the turtle was long gone.

"I can't, either. It's my first time."

Claire glanced around at him. "Really? You've never seen a turtle lay eggs before, even though you're from here?"

"I never have. Even though it's the season, it's still a little early, and it would be almost impossible to plan a time when a sighting would be guaranteed. I'm just glad our presence didn't deter her."

"Me, too."

He realized he was still leaning close to Rachel and immediately sat back. When he glanced at Marion, he noticed she was smiling, and even though she was looking in the direction of the ocean, he got the feeling her expression had nothing to do with the turtle.

Then what was it for?

Maybe the fact that he'd been practically leaning on her daughter?

If so, he needed to be careful. He didn't want to give Rachel's mom any ideas. Or worse, he didn't want Rachel to get any ideas.

So from here on out, he would need to be careful. Not just for his sake. But for everyone's.

Claire still wanted to say goodbye to Sebastien. And today was the day.

Rachel and Seb had worked all night long, securing places for their critical patients. It hadn't been easy. Many of the other islands were also on high alert, and there was an air of uncertainty and tension in all the phone calls she'd made. Hospitalier had agreed to receive patients from Bora Bora and other islands in the event that the storm shifted yet again and hit somewhere other than Taurati.

But they'd done it. And Rachel felt better about where things now stood with the hospital.

She'd barely had time to go home and catch a few hours of sleep before her mom and Claire's flight left today. She felt weepy and out of sorts, and she knew it was due to the prospect of being separated from her daughter. But not just that. There'd been a weird sense of companionship as she and Seb worked together last night. She'd put it down to being tired and having witnessed that magical scene on the beach yesterday. But she needed to banish that feeling—and soon.

They arrived at the hospital, and Rachel dropped her mom and Claire off at the front door and then went to find a parking place. When she rejoined them, she wrapped an arm around her daughter's shoulders and they headed through the entrance. Claire looked a little silly in her thick cardigan and long pants in this heat, but it was still winter in Wisconsin, and she needed to be prepared for it when she got off the plane tomorrow. Hopefully by then the storm would dissipate and things could go back to normal.

Normal? Like Sebastien calling her *Rach* for the first time yesterday? She thought of him as Seb all the time, but it was because everyone seemed to call him that. To hear him shorten *her* name, though, had given it a kind of intimacy she was no longer used to.

And she wasn't sure she wanted to get used to it again. Claire's father had called her that, and so it jolted to hear it roll off the tongue of another man. Although Sebastien's tones had worked some kind of magic over her that Roy's voice never had.

She glanced up to see Seb coming across the large foyer area to meet them. Alarm bells went off in her head. Ugh! She hadn't quite prepared herself for seeing him again. She'd told him what time they were coming but assumed he would just wait in his office until they arrived. He shoved a lock of hair off his forehead, sending a shiver over her. It was a study in impatience and sexiness all rolled into one. And his white shirt accentuated his tanned skin and strong neck. Imagining that fabric sliding across that tattoo of a sea turtle on his shoulder did a number on her.

Not the time, Rachel.

He was here, and she needed to pull herself together. Maybe he didn't want them in his space. Except she'd been there all night long.

Only that had been all work and no play. Not like that night in her cabana. The thought made her stomach tank and edged her nerves back into the danger zone. "Hey, sorry you felt you had to come down to meet us."

"It was no problem. I wanted to." His attention shifted to her daughter. "Claire, how are you holding up?"

"I thought this storm wasn't going to happen. You guys said it might be heading somewhere else." Her voice shook.

She realized then that Claire's eyes were red-rimmed, too. Had she been crying in her room before they left? Oh, God, was she even doing the right thing by sending her away?

Yes. She and Sebastien still had work to do, and she would have a harder time doing that if she knew Claire was here and might be in trouble.

"I know, and it still may. But we can't just sit back and pretend it's not out there."

She was surprised at how good a job Sebastien was doing at being supportive rather than just placating her. The respect she already had for him grew into a seedling.

"I understand that. But I don't really want to leave. Grams and Mom think I should, though. What if that other island gets hit? Who will help them?"

Sebastien seemed to consider his next words. "We will, if we can. And I agree with your mom and grandmother. They want to know you're safe and with the people you love. And we'll be working hard over the next several days."

"I guess." Claire's arms went over her chest in a way that showed how dubious she was about going. "There are people that I love here, too, though."

Rachel swallowed at the way her daughter had worded that. She knew that Claire liked Sebastien, but her daughter made it sound like he was inside that bubble of people she cared about. *Really* cared about. Claire had always had an open heart that never seemed to run out of compassion and empathy. Rachel liked that most of the time. But someday she was going to let someone in who would hurt her. Roy hadn't been there long enough to do any real harm to Claire when he'd left. But she'd asked about him, and Rachel had tried to answer her questions as honestly as possible, telling her they'd both been very young when they'd been together and Roy hadn't been ready to fully commit to her. She'd left out the part about him not wanting to be a father. But someday her daughter was probably going to want to track him down. What if Roy rejected her? How long could Rachel really protect her from that?

She couldn't. But she could try to protect her from getting too attached to this particular man. "I know you do, honey. But this isn't goodbye forever. It's just until this storm is no longer a threat."

Like the threat that Sebastien posed?

He's not, Rachel. You're comparing apples with oranges.

That cyclone could become an unstoppable force of nature, whereas Sebastien… Well, they could walk away from him at any time.

At least she hoped they could.

Marion gave her granddaughter a hug. "You're acting like this is a kidnapping, honey. This is not just about the storm. I've missed you. Just come home with me for a week, and then I'll bring you back myself, okay? You've always loved staying with us. Gramps would be really sad if I came back without you."

"I've missed you guys, too. It'll just seem strange for Mom and…er…my friends to be so far away."

"You have your cell phone. You can call her every day. This week will go by faster than you can imagine."

Claire's eyes shifted back to Seb. "Will you take care of my mom? Please?"

Horror went through Rachel, and she was quick to take away any notion that she needed anyone to do that. "I'm a big girl, Claire. I can take care of myself. Sebastien has his own family to think about."

She had no idea whether or not Sebastien's parents were even alive. He could have been raised in foster care for all she knew.

The pediatrician's jaw tightened visibly. Probably in response to Claire's outrageous request.

But other than that outward tell, Seb gave no indication that he was irritated.

"She and I will be working together every day, so if I see something I disapprove of, should I call you?"

Rachel's head whipped around, and she fixed him with a gaze that that told him to watch his step.

"Could you?" Claire responded.

"I'm sure your mom will be just fine." Marion glanced down at her phone. "Well, it's that time. We'd better get going, kiddo."

"Okay." Claire came over and gave Rachel a long hug. "I miss you already."

Clenching her jaws together to keep control of her emotions, she squeezed her daughter tight. "I'll miss you more. Be good, okay?"

"I'll try. I'll call you when we get to Tahiti. And when we get to Wisconsin."

"I'll be waiting." Dropping a kiss onto Claire's head, she finally released her.

Unexpectedly, her daughter went over to Seb and hugged him as well. There was a moment's hesitation before Sebastien's arms went around her back. Over Claire's head, his eyes met Rachel's with an odd expression. Almost like… sadness. A lump formed in her throat that no amount of swallowing would dislodge.

Seb took a step back and repeated what Rachel had said. "Be good. See you in a week."

Said like a father. Like the father that Claire had never had. It would be so easy to lean on him for support, just like she had when he'd treated Claire for her swollen lymph node.

This could turn into a disastrous situation for all of them. And yet he'd said nothing wrong. Any friend or neighbor could have said the same thing and she wouldn't have thought a thing of it.

Was it because it came from a man she'd slept with?

Probably.

But to overreact would make both Claire and Sebastien wonder about the reason behind it. And in reality, Rachel had no idea why her thoughts and emotions were in such turmoil.

It's because your daughter is about to fly thousands of miles away.

For the first time, she wondered if moving to Taurati had been the best idea. Then she shook that thought aside. It was, actually. Because she was far enough away from home that if things got too weird with Sebastien, or if she developed some kind of crush on the man, she could simply pick up and move house. It had been a lot more complicated when Roy had left, since he'd come from the same Wisconsin town as they had. And although his parents had been killed in a car crash soon after they graduated from college, his romance with Rachel had continued. At least until Claire was born and he decided fatherhood wasn't for him. He'd stayed in town for a couple of months after that before moving to one of the larger cities just north of them.

But there'd always been that specter of fear. What if he decided to move back to the area? What if he decided to lay claim to Claire or said he wanted to forge some kind of relationship with her? What if Claire decided she wanted a relationship with him?

It all seemed unlikely at this point, but she still worried about it. And when Claire turned eighteen, she could decide for herself what to do about that. All Rachel could do now was to protect her daughter as best she could.

And that might not be just from her biological father anymore. More and more she was realizing that Claire craved what she hadn't had as a baby—the fairy-tale notion of two parents who loved each other.

God, she didn't want to be the one who had

to smash that fantasy to bits in front of her daughter.

Sebastien broke the silence. "Hey, I have something for you in my office. Do you have a minute to come up?"

Claire looked at her grandmother, eyes wide. "Can we?"

"Yes, just for a minute, though."

"It won't take long."

They took the elevator to the third floor and stepped off. Rachel had no idea what Sebastien was talking about. He'd never mentioned having anything for Claire. But her anxiety levels were starting to climb higher and higher.

Seb opened the door to his office and ushered them in. And then, going behind his desk, he opened a drawer and pulled out a small plastic item. "It's a sea turtle. Something to help you remember Taurati."

His French accent came through thicker than it normally did.

Claire accepted the gift, turning it over in her hands. "Thank you. Just like the one we saw on the beach. I've always loved sea turtles."

"So did…" Sebastien let the words trail away for a minute before finishing it. "So do I. Think you can fit that in your backpack?"

"I'm going to put it in my purse for safekeeping." She looked at Seb. "I'll give it back to you when we come back."

"No, it's yours."

"Are you sure?"

"I am." He gave her a smile.

"Thank you. I love it. I'll put it on a shelf in my room when I come home."

Rachel's misgivings went even higher. But it wasn't as if he'd gifted her something expensive. It was probably just some trinket left by a patient of his, and he'd offered it to Claire to take away some of her anxiety.

Something whispered to her in the deepest recesses of her brain. Something about a turtle. She tried to capture it, but it slid away before she could.

She didn't want to take the chance that Claire would hug him again or form an even closer bond to him, so she interrupted the moment. "Well, you guys better be on your way. I love you. Call me when you land at each of your stops, okay?"

"Don't worry, we will." Marion kissed her cheek, then held her hand out to Seb. "Thank you. For everything. I can see why you treat children. You're very good with them."

"Thank you. It's just the training." Again there was something in his tone that called to her. Like when he'd looked at her while hugging Claire.

"I don't believe that for a second," her mom said.

Rachel didn't believe it, either. She'd seen him with his patients. He was kind and intuitive and seemed to have a gift for helping them calm down.

"I'll walk you out," she said.

Her mom shook her head. "It's probably better if we just go from here. Claire already has her backpack, and I have my things in my whale of a purse. We'll call you when we land, so don't worry. And you be careful."

The admonition was made with love, and Rachel knew it. She gave them each one more hug and then watched as they walked out the door. She stood there staring at it for a long minute before realizing tears were coursing unchecked down her cheeks.

A hand grasped hers and squeezed. "It's going to be okay, Rach. I promise."

Something about those words made a rush of emotion sweep into her head, where it grew and swelled until she felt her skull would split open. She whirled around to face him, not bothering to swipe at the moisture on her cheeks.

What did he know about promises?

"Don't. Just don't. You can't know that. So don't make any promises you can't keep."

He searched her face for a long moment. "You're right, and I'm sorry. I'm the last person who should be telling you that everything will be all right. Since I know firsthand that sometimes it's not, no matter how much you might wish otherwise."

CHAPTER SEVEN

WHY HAD HE said that?

He had no idea. But once the words were out of his mouth, he couldn't retract them. And he wouldn't even if he could after seeing the anguish on her face. But at least her separation from her daughter wasn't forever.

When she'd turned suddenly, she hadn't let go of his hand. And her grip was strong and fierce. As if, despite her angry words, she needed to hold on to something—even if it was a fake promise.

"You said you know firsthand. How?"

He had a choice. He could evade the question by acting like he was talking about one of his patients. But he didn't want to do that. And unlike the faceless acquaintances who cut his hair and backed away from the subject almost as soon as they asked that fateful question about children, he had a feeling she wouldn't. And he had no idea why.

"I had a son who died."

There was silence for several seconds, her eyes searching his as if working through what he'd said.

"Oh, God, I should have realized." Her head tilted, fingers tightening further around his. "That sea turtle. It's like the one on your shoulder. That toy didn't belong to a patient, did it?"

"No."

"Oh, Seb. I am so sorry. I had no idea." Her mouth twisted. "I remember implying that only someone with children could understand what it was like to worry about them. Only you did know, didn't you?"

He remembered that moment with shocking clarity. She hadn't used those exact words, but he'd been right about her meaning. "Not your fault. I rarely tell anyone about him."

A couple of beats passed in silence.

"Can I ask what happened? If you don't want to tell me, I'll completely understand."

He shouldn't want to tell her. He'd actually never *wanted* to tell anyone. Until now.

But this was Rachel. Someone who'd feared for her own daughter's life. If he could trust anyone to understand, it was her.

"He died of brain cancer when he was a year old."

A thousand emotions went through her eyes.

And he was right. She would understand exactly what it was like to hear the terrible words *Your child has cancer.*

She took a step closer. "Tell me."

And so he did. Told her how his baby's eyes had stopped looking into his. How he regressed on his milestones. How he became more and more difficult to console. And finally the results of that MRI that dropped the last of the puzzle pieces into place.

The process of telling Bleu's story was both terrible and cathartic. He talked until he had no more words.

"I never would have guessed. You've always seemed so…optimistic. Even when talking about this storm."

"It was either that or give in to the grief and go in a direction that helped no one. But believe me, I remember him each and every day of my life."

"Oh, Seb." She grasped his other hand and held it. "What was his name?"

"Bleu Zacharie Deslaurier."

"Bleu. I should have guessed." The words were soft, almost a whisper and said with a reverence that surprised him. "I remember tracing that on your shoulder a year ago."

A ball of emotion gathered in his stomach. "Yes. I remember, too."

He remembered her soft finger as it wound around letter after letter of his son's name. How it had sent a shuddery sense of familiarity through him, as if she'd spoken Bleu's name aloud, rather than just tracing it. It had been hypnotic. And so, so seductive.

Then. And now.

"I'm so glad you told me."

She was. He could see it in her face.

Before he could stop himself, he carried both of her hands to the small of her back and took a step toward her. Her head tipped back to look at him, and he was lost. There was no surprise in her gaze. No hint of rejection.

Instead, there was a warmth that drew him in until his body made contact with hers. And then slowly, slowly, his head lowered until his mouth connected with hers.

It was paradise. The taste. The feel.

Her lips were soft. So very soft.

In an instant, all rational thought fled, and all that existed was feeling. Physical feeling and a sense of being welcomed home, but it was more than that. There was an emotional connection he wasn't sure he'd ever felt before, even with Layla.

Using her hands, he applied slight pressure to ease her even closer, and she made a sound against his mouth. Some strange melding that was half groan, half purr. It sent raw heat pulsing through him.

Her mouth opened, and just like her gaze had earlier, it drew him in. His tongue filled the space, finding a moist heat that blanked every thought from his head. He wanted her. Wanted her like he'd never wanted anyone before.

Just like last time, when they'd…

Last time.

Merde. He'd promised her it would be all right. But if he went any further, it wouldn't be. This wasn't just about him and Rachel. She had a daughter that he didn't want drawn into the mix.

Letting go of her hands in a rush, he took a step back. Then another. It took a second for their mouths to unfuse, but when they did, he immediately regretted it.

She pressed the back of her hand to her lips, and she suddenly looked lost. More lost than she'd looked when saying goodbye to her mother and daughter. His gut clenched, and he had to press his fists to his sides to keep from reaching for her again.

"Rach…"

"No." She edged toward the door. "Don't say anything. I need to go. Need to get to work. I'm already late. So, so late."

With that, she opened the door and fled his

office, leaving him to stare after her. And to wonder if he hadn't just done the most selfish thing of his life by burying his grief in that kiss. There'd been no thoughts of storms or how hard it must have been for Rachel to send her only child away.

Or maybe that's what drove him to kiss her. He knew exactly what it was like to send off a child into the unknown. Knew how heart-wrenching and helpless it felt to say goodbye. But whatever had driven that crazy impulse, he needed to somehow make it right and move forward. The problem was he had no idea how.

Sleep seemed like a foreign concept to Rachel when she went home to an empty house. She lay on her back and stared up at the ceiling. God! She'd been so sure that Seb was going to lay her down on his couch and kiss all her worries away.

Except those worries would have grown exponentially afterward. So no matter how shocked she'd been when he stopped, no matter how quivery her legs were as she'd exited his office, he'd done her a favor by not going any further.

Because he was thinking. Unlike you, Rachel.
She wasn't even entirely sure how that kiss

had come about. But something inside her had melted when she grasped the fact that he'd given Claire his dead son's sea turtle to help her feel better. It was probably the same toy that had driven him to get that tattoo on his shoulder. In that moment of realization, she'd have given him anything.

Anything!

Maybe even her heart. And what a disaster that would have been. She needed to somehow get her head back on straight. He'd done an impulsively kind thing by giving away that turtle, but it hadn't really meant anything. Maybe he had all kinds of toys and mementos at home.

But the only one tattooed on his body was a sea turtle.

She hadn't asked him about Bleu's mother. She hadn't even thought about it, really. But she was sure if the mother of his child was still in his life, there was no way he would have been caught dead kissing someone else. She didn't know how she knew it, but she did.

And that gave her a sense of relief. And sadness.

Because in the end, who had held him during those moments of grief? And they still happened, from what she saw in his eyes. The thought of him at home alone, picturing his baby's smile...

God!

She turned onto her other side, punching her pillows a couple of times, and glanced at the clock. Two in the morning. Great.

She would more than likely see the man at work today, and she had no idea how she was going to face him. What she was going to say.

At least Claire would be safe. They'd made it to Tahiti, and their flight to Wisconsin was eleven hours, not including a three-hour layover in Chicago. But since it was an overnight flight, they could at least sleep. Unlike her.

But she'd better make an effort, or she was going to have a hard time keeping her mind on task tomorrow.

She called out to her smart device. "Eureka, find tropical rain forest sounds."

Grimacing, she gave a quick laugh. Well, it was better than asking it to find storm sounds. While she normally loved falling asleep to the sound of rain and thunder, she didn't want to send out any kind of subliminal message to the tropical storm that it was okay to come their way. Because it wasn't. She wanted it to stay as far away as possible.

The predictions were for Tropical Cyclone Koji to intensify even more overnight.

And somehow that seemed like it would solidify things in her mind. While the island could still be in danger. She definitely *was* in danger. From more than just this storm.

Well, she was going to have to push through and do her job. Because there were lives at stake. And she couldn't afford to give in to her heart and throw a massive pity party. That could wait.

With that last thought, she forced her eyes to close and prayed that sleep would finally find her and that she would not dream about that kiss. Or about anything else that involved Seb.

Something startled her awake, and for a second she lay in the dark, trying to figure out if it had been the strange dream she'd been having of Seb and running as fast as her legs would carry her. But she hadn't been running away from him. She'd been running toward him, could just see him in the distance, could almost touch his hand, when...

What?

The sound happened again, and she realized it was her cell phone. Glancing at the clock, she saw that it was five in the morning. Her first thought was Claire.

Sitting straight up, she reached for the phone that was on its charger. It wasn't Claire. She sagged for a moment before she realized it was Seb.

Oh, no! Calling to tell her not to bother coming in to work today? No, he wouldn't do that. No matter what had transpired between them, he wasn't unprofessional.

"'Lo?" The word didn't come out right, and her voice was gravelly and sleep filled. She cleared it and tried again. "Hello?"

"Rachel? Sorry to call so early, but there's news on the cyclone, and it's not good."

"Is it going to hit Taurati after all?"

"It doesn't look that way. It's going to make landfall in the next couple of hours. And Mauhali is set to get the brunt of it."

She blinked trying to get her groggy brain to work. "Is that the island they'd predicted?"

"No. It swung north a few hours ago. Mauhali is one of the poorest of the islands. Its population is on the lower end, and its health care is just the basics. They're not equipped to deal with a disaster like this."

"Got it. Give me a few minutes to get dressed, and I'll be there."

"Thanks. And, Rachel, I…"

"What?"

"Nothing. I'll just see you when you get here."

Seb was running on fumes.

He'd already fielded calls from Mauhali and

Neves, asking what the plan was. Not that he had a clue. They'd expected the possibility that patients could need to be evacuated to Taurati in front of the storm. But that the storm would hit Mauhali had not been on anyone's radar. There was no time for evacuations, since the winds were already picking up on the island ahead of the storm. And the storm would basically sit between their island and the other one.

Merde!

He hated calling Rachel in. Not just because of that kiss, but because he knew she was dealing with making her daughter leave, and if she was like him, she hadn't gotten much sleep last night. But it wasn't for much longer. Just until Koji was gone and they'd figured out what resources there were for Mauhali, and then they could go back to their respective corners of Pediatrics.

Was he ready for that?

Maybe not. Maybe the real question was: Was it a better situation?

And the answer to that question was probably yes. Even though, after telling Rachel about Bleu, there'd been a feeling of peace. As if he'd finally been able to lay his son to rest. It made no sense, but it was probably what had led to him kissing her in the first place. The whole rush of relief in finally being able to share what he'd gone through during Bleu's illness and death. He hadn't been able to reveal the depth of his grief with Layla, and they'd been engaged to be married. But that engagement had been more about the pregnancy than it had about love. He could see that now. But if Bleu had lived, he could also see that he would have worked damned hard to make things work.

Seb hunched over his computer monitor, trying to figure out what that next step might be. Whatever it was, it would now take place after the storm had passed.

He got up to stretch for a minute and then decided to grab a coffee before Rachel arrived.

Heading out the door, he rounded the corner to the elevator and stopped. Rachel. She was already here at the hospital. Talking to Philippe Chauvre. Whatever she'd said made him smile, and he reached out to touch her arm.

She smiled back, and Seb tensed.

Was the man asking her out?

And if he was, it was none of his business, although a little spiral of something in his brain called Seb a liar.

When Rachel's head turned and saw him, her smile disappeared, a look of utter guilt appearing in her eyes.

Hell. He wasn't trying to make her feel bad. Or feel anything, really.

He made his way over to them, nodded at Philippe and turned his attention to her. "I'm headed for coffee. Want anything?"

"I—I…ran into Philippe on the way to your office."

He hadn't asked. Maybe she felt guilty for getting sidetracked. But he knew Philippe enough to know there was almost no walking past him without having a conversation.

A part of Seb might not like her getting chummy with the orthopedist, but he wasn't involved with Rachel, and he had no right to feel one way or the other about it.

Rachel was a beautiful woman—why should he be surprised that he wasn't the only one to notice that?

But he wasn't going to stand here and interrupt whatever this was. He needed to go get his coffee so they could finish their conversation in peace.

And if the man was asking her out?

Again, none of his business.

Before Seb could move away from the pair, though, the orthopedic surgeon smiled at him. "I guess I got caught red-handed."

The statement took him by surprise. "Sorry?"

"I came up here to lure Rachel away from you."

Damn! Had she told the man about that kiss? Or worse, implied that Seb was interested in her?

He wasn't, no matter how that kiss had looked. It had been impulsive and stupid, and he was damned sure not going to do anything like that again.

Rachel drew what looked to be an overly careful breath. "He means lure me away from Pediatrics."

Ah, hell. His imagination was going to get the best of him. Of course it hadn't been about anything that had happened yesterday.

"A position just opened up in my department and—"

He didn't need to hear any more. "There's a storm out there, Philippe. Can't this wait?"

The man had the grace to look chagrined. "Of course it can. I just happened to get on the elevator with her and asked if she had a minute."

Rachel stared at Seb like he had two heads. But she was seriously thinking of leaving Pediatrics?

Hell, he'd just been thinking about how much better it would be when they were no longer working together. So wouldn't that kind of move be the perfect solution?

Maybe, but he didn't like it. He and Philippe were both heads of their respective departments. He'd never tried to "lure"—as the other man had put it—anyone away from their position.

He decided to leave it. For now. Because what he'd said was true. There was a storm out there, and this was no time for hospital politics. He forced a smile. "So, about that coffee…"

Philippe shrugged. "I think that's my signal to head back to my own department." He touched Rachel's arm again. "Think about it, though, okay?"

Rachel didn't have a chance to say anything before the other man turned and pressed the button for the elevator.

Wanting to make sure that kiss had nothing to do with the conversation, he said, "Are you unhappy in Pediatrics?"

"No. He mentioned it when that chain saw accident came through the ER and I was helping him during surgery. We really did meet in the elevator. He didn't seek me out for a meeting or anything."

If he'd been worried about that kiss carrying too much meaning, he evidently needn't have. Philippe had a reputation for being competitive, claiming his team was one of the hospital's best. It made sense if Rachel had impressed him in some way that he'd tried to persuade her to join his team.

Would Rachel think about the offer and decide it was what she wanted to do?

Not something he was going to ask. So he decided to repeat his earlier question. "It's fine. You drink espresso, if I remember right."

She looked surprise. "I do. And that sounds great. I just jumped out of bed and dragged my clothes on, so I didn't even get my morning coffee."

Rachel didn't look like she'd just dragged her clothes on. The morning after they'd slept together a year ago, her hair had been beautifully rumpled and sexy, and he almost hadn't been able to leave.

None of that was evident now. Her hair was neatly pulled up into a clip, whatever messiness there might have been neatly twisted away.

"I'll get you one, and I'll be right back, if you want to wait in my office."

"Sounds good, thanks."

She'd dreamed about him.

Rachel wandered around Seb's office, waiting for him to get back from the coffee shop. His space was neat and organized, just like the other times she'd been in here. On his whiteboard were some facts about the storm.

The name *Mauhali* was at the top and had been underlined several times. Next to it were some facts and statistics about the island. Including the one community health clinic that was housed on the island. There was a helicopter pad, but no real airport.

She hadn't even stopped to listen to the news this morning. And then as she was rushing up to his office, Philippe had waylaid her talking again about the possibility of her moving to Ortho. And like the other doctor had said, they'd gotten caught red-handed.

She'd finally drifted off to sleep but then had had strange fitful dreams. Seb had called her just as her hand was reaching out to grab him in her dream.

Was that her subconscious trying to tell her something? That she was grabbing at something that wasn't in her or Claire's best interest?

Was Philippe's request the universe's way of telling her to get out while she could—before she got entangled in a situation that would only bring her heartache?

No. If she took that job, it wouldn't be because she was running from something. It would be because she thought it was something she'd be good at. Something that would be rewarding in its own right.

Sebastien came back before she had a chance to think through any of it. He was carrying two cups, one of them a disposable paper container and the other a china cup emblazoned with the Centre Hospitalier's name.

Her head tilted. "You could have had mine put in a disposable cup, too."

"I think I remember you saying you didn't care for the taste they gave your coffee."

He remembered that? A shiver of warmth went through her, which reminded her of her dream.

Don't grab at him.

"Well, thank you. But I've drunk plenty of coffee in paper cups and survived the experience." She smiled and took the proffered cup. "Besides, I'm surprised they let you carry this out of the cafeteria."

His lips curved. "Philippe's not the only one who can be persuasive."

Was he saying that the china cup was his way of persuading her to stay in Pediatrics? Or was it just like it sounded—that he'd talked the cafeteria staff into letting him take one of their cups?

The latter, obviously. To read anything else into it was ridiculous.

She decided not to bite, instead saying, "Well, thanks for the coffee."

"Yep. Ready to get to work?"

When she nodded, taking her first sip and savoring the strong brew, he pulled up a map with projections. "This is where things stand right now."

Her eyes scanned the red cone that fanned out from the storm. A storm that was already far too close to shore. Wind speeds were... She swallowed hard. They stood at a hundred miles an hour. "That looks a lot different from what it was last night when I went to bed."

She didn't tell him how long it took her to actually fall asleep.

"Yes, it does. Neves want to meet with us to discuss how Hospitalier can take advantage of the work we've already done. Especially since Taurati is now officially off the critical list. It looks like Mauhali will be the worst hit of the islands, although the outer bands may skate across Bora Bora before it slides back out to open water." He stared at the screen. "Bora Bora has good infrastructure, whereas Mauhali...well, it doesn't. It's known for its mango exports, so there are extra workers there, who I imagine are trying to get everything off the trees they can now before the storm decimates the harvest. So they may not have evacuated even if they were urged to."

"And the population?"

"Right now, we're probably looking at a thousand."

"That's a lot of potential patients."

"It is. And another problem is the helipad's a little distance from the clinic, due to the topography of the island."

"So we're looking at a task that might very well be..."

"Impossible." He finished the sentence for her. "Yes, but if we can coordinate any medevac with other islands and schedule landings, it could work. Neves says they're asking for a team from the hospital to go as soon as the winds die down a bit. So we need get that started, too."

She glanced over at him, noting he had some dark circles going on under his eyes. She wasn't the only one who hadn't gotten a good night's sleep, evidently.

"Have you been up all night?"

"I happened to wake up and looked at the weather. I called you and Neves right after I saw it."

Well, at least he hadn't left her out of the equation.

"When does he want to meet?"

"As soon as we can. Let me see if he's arrived yet." Seb retrieved his phone and dialed the hospital administrator's number. "Hi, are you at the hospital?"

He glanced at Rachel. "Yep, she's here, too.

Are you ready for us?" There was a pause. "Okay, we'll be right there."

At Neves's office, they discussed what they could do for Mauhali and who should be on the team that went to the island. They decided on four people, since there was only so much they could do on-site, medically. They'd take basic supplies, but surgeries there would be next to impossible to do. As well as Rachel and Seb, the team would consist of Dr. Monchamp, one of the ER doctors with military training, and a nurse called Kayla Courrier, who would help with triage and identifying the most critical patients. Dr. Monchamp and Kayla would stay on the island and help coordinate who went on which chopper. And she and Seb would ride back and forth on the chopper that would ferry patients to Hospitalier.

"I need you guys to stay in close contact with the hospital, so we know what's coming in."

She nodded. Lord, she hoped she was ready for this. But Neves wouldn't be sending them out if he wasn't confident in their abilities. And although she was a pediatric nurse now, she'd once been involved with search-and-rescue teams right after finishing her nursing degree.

"We'll get the hospitals lined up, since we already know who has choppers and who has space in their facilities."

"Okay. Go. Give me a buzz when you get ready to go. I imagine we still have quite a bit of waiting to do."

Almost twelve hours' worth. Maybe more by the time the last of the bands crossed Mauhali.

The next several hours were spent getting hospitals onboard with their plans, which was easy, since everyone was eager to help out. Only one hospital couldn't, since they'd had an outbreak of norovirus from one of the cruise ships. They were barely keeping their heads above water.

Just as she got off a call, her phone buzzed. She glanced down just as Seb looked over at her. "It's Claire." She pushed a button to answer.

"Hi, honey. Did you guys make it?"

"Yes. Just wanted to let you know that we're at Grams's house."

She sent Sebastien a thumbs-up sign. "I'm glad you made it."

Claire's voice came through. "Did you hear that Taurati isn't going to be hit?"

"We did. But it's going to hit another island, so we're trying to get some plans together."

"You promised you'd help them."

It was so like Claire to remember everything, even things she wished her daughter would forget. "We're going to fly over once the storm has passed. And yes, we'll help however we can."

"Good. And I miss you already."

"I miss you, too, sweetheart."

"Tell Sebastien that I miss him, too."

She swallowed, but what choice did she have but to agree? "Okay, I'll tell him."

"And that his turtle made it through customs without any problem."

Rachel held her hand over the phone when she realized Seb's head had tilted when he realized they were probably talking about him. "She said to tell you that the turtle made it through without being confiscated." She made no mention of what else Claire had said.

He smiled. "Good news."

"Okay, honey, tell Grams we'll call you guys when we get on the chopper for Mauhali." Too late she realized she'd used the word *we*, meaning her and Seb. But there was no way to correct it without it becoming very awkward, so she just let it go.

"Okay. We'll be watching the news."

"Love you, honey. Tell Grams and Gramps, too."

"I will. 'Bye."

With that, she hung up the phone.

"They're doing okay, I take it?"

She smiled. "Better than we are, I think. I'm

really glad Claire went back with my mom. And you were right. It would have been too hard to work with her and my mom sitting either at home or here at the hospital worrying about every movement that storm made." She paused. "What happened here during Wasa-Arthur?"

"They rode it out, for the most part. There were surprisingly few fatalities. But they were good about evacuating people from the coastal areas to the interior. That helped a lot."

"Is that what will happen on Mauhali?"

"That island is a lot smaller than Taurati. So the interior of that island is not super far from the coastline. A lot of them will probably shelter in place. But some will move inland. If they can."

She nodded and sat back down. "I need to make some more calls and see if I can make more of those connections we were talking about."

"I'll do the same."

If it came down to it, maybe Rachel would do what the rest of the islanders did, according to Seb. She'd just find a place to hunker down and hope for the best.

CHAPTER EIGHT

"WE NEED TO get some sleep. Is there anything you need from home? I'm afraid it's going to be an early morning." It was after eleven, and they'd been working nonstop all day.

Koji was on the shores of Mauhali, the first of its bands already wreaking havoc on the tiny island.

"I brought a tote bag with me, just in case."

"Okay, good. The couch pulls out into a bed."

She blinked, one side of her mouth going up in amusement. "Well, that takes care of one of us."

He laughed. "Don't worry. I wasn't planning on sharing it with you. I'll be quite comfortable in one of the chairs."

"Even a chair sounds heavenly right now." She stood and stretched.

Locks of hair had fallen free from her clip and scattered around her face in waves. She was beautiful. In more ways than one. And working with her today had been surprisingly easy. Something he hadn't expected, given their past. And given that kiss that now seemed like forever ago.

"Why don't you take the bathroom first, while I get the bed made up?"

She regarded him for a second. "Are you sure you don't mind me sleeping here? I could probably go to the on-call room and grab some shut-eye."

"You probably would get a whole lot less sleep in there than you would here. You know what those are like."

"Unfortunately, I do." She picked up her bag. "I'll be quick."

He'd just finished throwing the covers over the bed when she came out, hair wet and smelling of that vanilla-and-coconut scent he'd come to associate with her. She was dressed in sweats and a large T-shirt, but hell, he couldn't stop picturing her in his small shower...naked. He knew he was going to have a hell of a time forgetting it from here on out.

"Thanks. I didn't realize you had an actual shower. I hope you don't mind."

"Of course not. Neither of us knows when we'll get our next one."

She tossed her bag on the bed. "It's all yours."

And none too soon. He nodded before turning and making his way in there. And he hoped beyond hope that he was actually going to be able to sleep, knowing she was mere feet away from him.

They both had a job to do. And the sooner he remembered that, the better off he would be.

It was still dark, but the readout on her phone said it was almost five. She could just make out Seb a few yards away. He'd evidently abandoned the chair in favor of the floor, the outline of a blanket beneath his body. He was on his stomach, both arms stretched above his head, the left one curving. He had jogging pants and a T-shirt on, but she could imagine the outline of his tattoo beneath it. In memory of his son. It was heartbreaking. And the sweetest thing she could imagine.

She forced her gaze away from him and surveyed the light that came in through the rectangular sliver of a window on his door. The takeout boxes from last night were all gone. He must have cleaned up after he'd gotten out of the bathroom. She'd been going to do it, but the second she sat on that bed, exhaustion pulled at her. She figured she'd just do it in the morning.

Except he'd already done it.

She tried to pull up the news stories on her

phone, but the light must have disturbed Seb, because his voice broke through the silence.

"How long have you been up?"

"About five minutes. I'm just trying to find out what's happening with the storm."

A few minutes later, they sat at his computer. There was no news from Mauhali that they could see, but the storm was almost gone. The last band was just now sweeping through, and wind speeds had been downgraded to a level-one tropical cyclone.

Koji was weakening.

Thank God. But how much damage had it caused?

"I'm going to see if I can rouse our team and get things underway. I'm hoping we can be airborne as soon as the wind speeds are down."

They were in the air an hour later. It had been forever since she'd been in a helicopter, and the closer they got to the island, the worse the winds became, buffeting the small aircraft. Dr. Felix Monchamp and Kayla Courrier were seated behind them. A small medical area at the back of the chopper was ready for up to two patients, or one if the patient was in critical condition. The mayor of Mauhali had declared a state of emergency. There had been no deaths reported yet, but almost every road was blocked by debris.

A particular bit of turbulence dropped the aircraft for a few seconds before they continued on their way. Rachel's fingers scrabbled for a handhold so she didn't end up in Seb's lap.

From behind her, Kayla moaned. "Ooh, my stomach."

She could relate. She would be glad when they were on the ground. By the time they took off again, hopefully the winds would be less of an issue. She could see why they hadn't gotten air clearance until just now.

A hand covered hers. "You okay?"

She nodded, tossing him a smile. "I've been on a couple of rescues before, but never with quite this much wind. How close are we?"

"About another fifteen minutes, and we should be there."

Seb let go of her hand to turn and speak to the two other team members, and she immediately missed the contact.

Stress. It had to be. It had nothing to do with the fact that he'd looked so peaceful and approachable sleeping on the floor this morning. Or the fact that they'd been working so closely together for almost a week. It seemed so much longer than that. Kind of like time had stretched out into a month's worth of encounters. And realistically, it was probably more than the amount of time they would have spend together over a month. And they certainly wouldn't have shared meals or watched that sea turtle together like a...

Like a family.

No. Don't keep thinking of him like that. He is not family, nor will he ever be.

For the next fifteen minutes, she forced herself to think of the movements of the helicopter and about what they might face when they finally landed. Anything that would keep her from mulling over things that not only seemed impossible but *were* impossible.

The first thing she saw when they set down on the helicopter pad were mangoes. So many mangoes. They were scattered across the clearing like tiny beach balls. And the second the door to the chopper opened, a strange smell assaulted her nostrils, and it was all she could do to keep herself from grimacing. It was a cloyingly sweet mixture of fruit, seaweed and dead fish. She saw why a few feet away, where a huge fish lay unmoving, evidently washed ashore by the force of the storm.

"God," she whispered as she stepped out of the helicopter and peered around her. Downed trees and debris had been flung everywhere.

Not too far from them, some kind of building hunched as if in pain, missing its roof, while one side of the structure had collapsed inward. All thoughts of minor discomforts from the trip over or woes about Seb immediately vanished.

This was the look of utter devastation.

A man hurried toward them, his hair blown about by the slowing rotors of the helicopter. Even when the blades stopped, the wind continued. He said something in Tahitian that she didn't understand, until Seb translated it for her. "He's asking us to come to the clinic. They have some injuries that need immediate care. The physician assistant who basically runs the clinic is one of the injured."

The fact that the man was on foot told them that vehicles were not moving freely. They'd probably been lucky to be able to land.

Seb nodded and responded to him. Then he turned to them. "Let's get our gear and two stretchers. The clinic wasn't totally demolished, so we can use whatever supplies are there, although power is out."

It wasn't until they'd picked their way through the streets that the man introduced himself as Ari'i Teriyong, the mayor of Mauhali.

By the time the small community clinic came within sight, Rachel was perspiring, and her hair hung in damp hanks around her head. They'd had to pick their way around trees and debris on almost every road they'd traveled down. With the stretchers being awkward to carry, it slowed their progress. She glanced at Seb to see he still looked a whole lot better than she felt. His hair looked shiny and clean and definitely wasn't sticking to his head like hers was.

She heard the familiar cries of people in pain as they came out of a stand of trees that opened to the clinic. Two of the windows had been blown out by the force of the storm, and there was glass everywhere, but the structure itself was still intact. The scene was one of chaotic order. People sat outside the building, and a couple were lying on blankets nearby.

The team went to work, each person quickly moving from patient to patient to assess. She stuck close to Seb, since her Tahitian wasn't as good as it needed to be. Something she needed to get serious about if she was going to stay on the island.

Was she mentally keeping one foot planted in the States, not fully committing to Taurati? Maybe not consciously. But unconsciously? Claire had been diligent about studying both languages.

Sebastien immediately moved toward a child, who was crying and writhing in her mother's arms.

"Aidez-nous! Aidez-nous!"

The words were in French, and these she understood as a cry for help.

The little girl, who couldn't have been more than five, was wheezing, trying to catch her breath, crying with each exhale. Her face was a picture of pure panic. Seb called to Dr. Monchamp. "We need to treat this one."

"We're still assessing, so go."

They got a quick history from the girl's mom, who said Lara had been hit in the chest by their front door when it was blown off its hinges. She'd carried her all the way to the clinic from over a mile away. They'd arrived an hour ago. The terror in the woman's voice was one she recognized all too well from Claire's health crisis.

Rachel's heart clenched as tears coursed down the mom's cheeks while she whispered over the girl's cries, rocking her back and forth. She put a hand on the woman's shoulder to stop the motion, fearing it would hurt the child even more.

Seb's voice was steady and calm as he explained to the pair that they were going to have to examine her, and that the mom needed to stay as still as possible. Rachel knew exactly why. He didn't want to move the girl until he knew exactly what they were dealing with.

He touched the child's hand. "Where does it hurt?"

Through her cries she pointed at the right side of her chest, over her ribs.

"How about your back? Does that hurt?"

"Non." The second she had to breathe back in, she cried out.

A dark bruise on her cheek testified to the force with which she'd been hit by the door.

"I think her back is clear, so let's get a stretcher and lay her on it. She's going to need to be transported as soon as we can."

She was glad they'd taken the time to drag those things here. Once retrieved, Rachel laid it close to the mom's side while Sebastien held one of the child's hands. "Lara, we have to move you to the cot, okay?"

The girl shook her head, crying out again. *"Non! Non!"*

"I know it hurts, and we're going to try hard to make it better, but we have to look at your chest."

Again she shook her head, starting to whimper.

That there were broken ribs involved was almost a certainty with this level of pain. But she knew Seb couldn't give the child anything for the pain without knowing what they were dealing with. Narcotics tended to depress the respiratory system and could cause it to arrest.

Seb looked at Lara's mom, who seemed to understand his silent question. She nodded, her chest spasming as if suppressing her own sobs.

"On three. Rach, you support her lower half, and I'll do the upper. Let's keep from twisting her at all."

So he also thought there were ribs involved.

"Un, deux, trois..."

A bloodcurdling scream went up as they gingerly took the little girl from her mom's arms and laid her on the cot. The whole area went silent right afterward.

She glanced at Kayla and Dr. Monchamp and saw they hadn't looked up, leaning over a patient. Their focus and ability to block out what wasn't right in front of them was unlike anything she'd ever seen.

Rachel lifted the girl's top, and right away they saw the ribs on her right side were dark purple, looking worse than even her face. And as she breathed in, a section of her chest sank inward even as the rest of her ribs expanded. When she exhaled, the bruised section moved in the opposite direction. Paradoxical breathing. Not a good sign.

She swallowed. "Flail chest."

"I see it. We need to get her in the chopper immediately." He glanced at the mom. "Can you run in the clinic and see if you can find a pillow and a long strip of tape?"

The woman did as asked, coming back a minute later with a pillow and a box of gauze. "These?"

Sebastien nodded. "Yes, those are perfect, thank you."

"You're going to stabilize the flail?" Rachel asked.

"Yes, since we'll be carrying her on the stretcher. I don't want those broken ribs damaging her lungs as she's jostled on the way to the chopper."

Using a long strip of gauze, he slid it between her back and the cot. He glanced at Rachel. "You know what to do?"

"Yes."

She laid the pillow over the right side of Lara's body but didn't press on it yet. Even so, the girl moaned in pain.

Seb touched the girl's head. "I know it hurts. But can you take a deep breath and hold it?"

Through her tears, she did as asked, and then Rachel applied pressure with the pillow to the area that she knew was depressed. The second she did, the girl screamed again, exhaling everything she had just breathed in. But that was what they wanted. The pressure would keep the flail section from pushing up while the ribs were deflating. While Rachel held the pillow in place, Seb tied the gauze around the pillow tight enough to maintain pressure without restricting her breathing even further.

"We're all done," he said.

The girl gingerly took a couple of breaths.

"It should hurt a little less now. We're going to pick up the cot and carry you to a helicopter."

"Maman..."

"Your mom can come." Seb glanced up. "Can you? Or do you have other children you need to care for?"

"She is my only. I will of course come."

Seb nodded. "I'll be right back."

He went over to Dr. Monchamp, saying something to him, to which the other man nodded. When he came back, he had a couple of men with him. "They'll carry the cot in case we need to stop and take care of anything."

He didn't need to say what he was thinking. She already knew. It was in case Lara stopped breathing or arrested on the trip to the chopper.

They started out. The half-mile trip was grueling and tense, since each movement jostled those ribs and caused terrible pain.

But then they were there. While the pilot

started the aircraft, she got Lara's oxygen going, and Seb strapped the cot in place.

Then they were off.

They glanced at each other as the chopper flew, and Seb said, "Good work."

She gave him a half smile. "Ditto to you."

Lara's mom was crouched over her daughter, smoothing her hair and telling the girl something.

Rachel's brows went up in question.

Replying in English, he said. "She's talking about the brave doctors who came to help them."

With Lara now stabilized, her own lungs deflated as she released a huge ball of tension. "How were Kayla and Dr. Monchamp doing?"

"They have an emergency case as well, but a chopper is almost there from Bora Bora with a medical team, so they'll load her in and go back to caring for others."

"Do you know how many islands are included in the rescue efforts?"

"Mayor Ari'i said four."

"Thank God. I'm glad it's not just us."

Seb glanced down at the mom and daughter. "Me, too. But I'm glad we were able to be there."

"So am I."

Something unspoken seemed to pass between them, the touch of softness in Seb's glance making Rachel's chest clog. Then the moment passed, and they got back to work, calling the hospital and asking them to have a team ready to receive them.

They arrived at the hospital an hour later, and four medical staff members rushed toward them with a gurney. Within minutes, they got Lara off the chopper and were headed toward the door.

Seb ducked his head into the aircraft. "Do you have enough fuel for another trip?"

The pilot nodded. "I do. Then I'll need to refuel the next time we get back."

Seb glanced at Rachel. "Are you up for heading back to Mauhali?"

"Absolutely."

He smiled. "I was hoping you'd say that."

CHAPTER NINE

Two MORE CHOPPER trips and the clinic's clearing was finally empty, other islands having also transported the worst of the patients. Dr. Monchamp and Kayla both volunteered to stay onsite for a couple of days to help with the more minor injuries and to oversee the clinic getting the power restored via the generator.

The second they'd set down at the hospital for the last time and their patient had been transferred, he sighed before thanking the pilot. It had been a long day. But a very good one. To his knowledge not one of their patients had died, and there'd been no casualties on Mauhali. And the other islands that had gotten some of the stronger winds had come through pretty well.

He turned to Rachel.

Her hair was mussed in the best kind of way, although it looked like she'd dragged her fingers through it to try to get some semblance of order back into it. The clip she'd stuffed it into partway through the day was long gone, and her tresses hung long and free. She was beautiful, and working with her on the island had been…

Like nothing he'd ever experienced. She was strong and capable and had balked at nothing, including putting pressure on a flail chest and helping him stabilize it.

No wonder Philippe Chauvre wanted her on his team. Seb knew he didn't want to lose her.

In more ways than one?

That had to be the exhaustion talking. He realized he was just standing there and forced himself to speak.

"Thank you, Rach. For everything. Coffee?" Somehow, he didn't want her to go her separate way just yet.

"Yes, that sounds heavenly."

"The cafeteria is closed, but they let you do self-serve after hours."

Leaving the chopper pad and going into the building, she said, "Can you go on ahead so I can call Claire? I'll catch up with you."

"Okay, see you in a few minutes."

He went into the elevator just as he heard Rachel say, "Hello, sweetheart, how was your day?"

He swallowed past a lump in his throat. How

would it feel to have someone say those words to him?

His and Layla's relationship had been passionate, but looking back, he could see that their young love had been largely driven by hormones and a sense of infatuation. It was no wonder their relationship had disintegrated once Bleu was gone. He'd been their glue.

He got to the cafeteria and found one of the carafes still had coffee in it. He then glanced at the espresso machine next to it, perusing the knobs and settings with a frown. He knew that's what Rachel liked. But he also had no idea how to use the thing.

"Something I can help you with?" The voice from behind him was the one he'd heard repeatedly over the last week. And right now it was filled with amusement.

He turned to face her. "That was fast."

"I wanted to make sure she knew I was okay and that we had done what she asked us to do. I told her I'd call her tomorrow with details. Once I've had a chance to decompress. Starting with coffee."

He motioned at the espresso machine. "I was going to try to tackle that, but…"

"Here, you get your coffee, and I'll get mine."

He watched as she expertly packed coffee into some kind of large spoon-looking device and then twisted it onto the underside of the machine, setting a paper cup underneath. Then she pressed a button, and the machine made a bubbling sound, then hissed out a thin, dark stream of fragrant brew.

"See? Not so hard."

He chuckled. "Easy for you to say. Sorry they don't have any real cups out."

"It's okay. I'll survive."

For his, he picked up a carafe and poured. "Mine's a little easier to figure out," he joked.

"Yes, but is it as good? Sometimes the best things take a little effort. But the results are well worth it."

Sometimes it didn't matter how much effort went into something. The results weren't always perfect, like that dark, rich coffee. His son and his relationship with Layla were two examples of that.

But how much effort had he really put into anything after Bleu had died? He was realistic enough to know that he'd been pretty emotionally unreachable for a long time after that. Looking back, he couldn't blame Layla for making the choice she had. She'd probably needed him, and he hadn't been there. Or maybe she hadn't. What he did know was that he hadn't been willing to become that vulnerable with anyone for a long time. And he wasn't sure he was capable of it anymore. But working with Rachel like he had… It made him wonder. It was almost as if they'd anticipated each other's thoughts on treatment and had worked together seamlessly. It had come as a surprise. Maybe it had been the setting and the need for quick action. But what she'd said was true. The effort they'd put into those patients on Mauhali had been worth it in the end. But relationships? That was another story.

"I'm good with my no-effort choice." But was he really? Or had he just settled for what he was comfortable with? Like he'd done most of his life. Since his son's death, he'd very rarely stepped outside his comfort zone.

Why? Mauhali had been outside his comfort zone. And yet he was very glad he'd gone. Had been very glad to see his and Rachel's work on preparedness put to good use.

"Are you sure you don't want to at least try this? I'll even walk you through how to use the machine."

Her words weren't a challenge, necessarily, but maybe it was time he took that first step and tried something completely different. Like today had been.

Without a word he set his coffee down. "You're on. Teach me. But I can't promise I'll like it."

"No promise expected." She took a sip of her brew, then took the cup filter thing off the machine and pounded it on the side of a metal can labeled Used Grounds. Then she handed it to him while she took another sip.

She walked him through the process, correcting him when he didn't tamp the coffee into the reservoir hard enough. "It uses pressure to push water through the grounds, so they have to be tightly packed."

A minute later, the water hissed through the machine like it had done with Rachel's.

"There's sugar here. How sweet do you like it?"

There was something about the way she said that last phrase that caught him off guard, and he found himself saying, "I like a good balance between sweet…and not so sweet." He smiled. "So how much should I add for that?"

She grinned at him. "Maybe half a packet of sugar, since these are bigger than what we have in the States."

He dumped half of the sugar in and gave the concoction a quick stir. Then he sipped.

Okay. He'd expected it to taste like something akin to used motor oil, since it was as dark as that. But it didn't. It was strong, yes, but it had a body to it that his own coffee didn't have. A bite that slid across his tongue in just the right way.

"How is it?"

"Not as bad as I thought it might be."

Her brows went up. "Hmm…but is it *good*?"

He thought for a second as he gave it another try. "Yes. It is."

"And worth the effort?"

"The jury is still out on that." And it was. Not just about the coffee, either. But about a lot of things.

"I'll take it." She took one last drink, then crumpled her cup and tossed it.

He did the same. Then he picked up his regular-size cup of coffee. "Mine lasts a whole lot longer, though. So maybe that's where my coffee beats yours. Maybe the enjoyment of savoring the experience, down to the final drop, is what makes it so great."

She pursed her lips as if thinking. "But maybe leaving your mouth wanting more makes you look forward to the next time that much more."

He went very still. Were they still talking about coffee or about something else entirely?

She'd left him wanting more a year ago.

But that didn't mean they should pick up where they'd left off. Right?

But he could use some downtime after their frenetic time on Mauhali. And he found he didn't want to be alone with his thoughts right now. "Let's go sit out on the beach for a bit and clear our heads. Unless you want to go home and get some real rest."

"I'm too keyed up to sleep right now. And listening to the ocean while it's still quiet sounds like an amazing option."

Seb chugged the rest of his coffee down, and they headed for the exit. Warm air hit him as soon as they made it through the doors, the heat both familiar and foreign. You wouldn't know it from how still the air was that a powerful storm had just blown through an island similar to theirs. Leaving destruction in its wake.

"The stars are incredibly bright tonight."

He glanced up and saw she was right. The moon, along with thousands of pinpoints of light, were on clear display, the quiet flickering making for an ever-changing show. They were there, just as they always were. A reminder that no matter what, there were some things you could count on. "Yes, they are."

Picking their way across the boardwalk, they finally came out onto the sand, which was still warm from the day's sun. Rachel kicked off her shoes, burying her toes in the soft surface. Pink polish shone up from her tanned feet. It was a good combination.

The moon cast its light across the space,

making some of the individual grains of sand sparkle, adding to the mystical feel of the night. It was almost eerie how different it was from the day they'd had.

Still. Quiet. Peaceful.

They walked toward the water, and Rachel stepped into the low surf, fisting the fabric of her loose skirt up to her knees. "You know, I never considered myself a beach person before I came to Taurati. It just seemed like too much work with the sand and salt."

"Didn't you say a little while ago that some of the best things take a little effort?"

She laughed and kicked a bit of water his way. "Touché. But then again, it looks like I was right, because the ocean is definitely worth it." She glanced down the beach. "I can't imagine those cabanas being washed away, can you?"

"No. These are used for fishing and sight-seeing spots rather than overnight guests. The hospital pays for their upkeep. They're rustic, but the charm is definitely there."

"Yes, it is. I didn't realize the hospital owned them, though. I just assumed that they were part of a resort like the one I stayed in when…"

She didn't finish her sentence, but he could pretty much guess what she'd been about to say.

"No. The hospital had these four put in for the use of patients' families and staff. There have even been several small weddings held in them. You've never been inside one?"

"No. Like I said, I didn't know the hospital owned them." She smiled. "My French and Tahitian language skills could use some work."

"It just takes time." He tilted his head in that direction. "Come on. I'll show you one of the cabanas."

The last thing he wanted to do was go home. Despite the crazy day, he'd enjoyed spending it with her. He hadn't been in one of these cabanas in four years. It had been part of the tour the hospital had given him when he'd signed on at the center. He was surprised they hadn't done the same for Rachel.

While she continued to walk in the water, he stayed on the shore, making his way toward the first of the cabanas about a hundred yards down the coast.

There was something about the moonlight playing across the water and her dark hair that made his fingers itch to slide through it. He remembered exactly what it felt like. And the cabanas weren't helping, because they were bringing back memories that were quickly crowding his brain.

The thought of going into another one of them with her...

Maybe this was a mistake.

Hell, but even that thought wasn't enough to make him stop and call the tour off.

Just then she called out, "Hey." She came out of the water and grabbed his hand, pointing. "What's that?"

He turned and looked in the direction she'd indicated, her fingers warm and soft, just like they'd been as they skated over his body that night a year ago. He almost groaned aloud. He needed to cut it out.

She spoke again. "Is that where we saw the turtle?"

There was a flag stuck into the sand with a caution symbol and the words *Ne Pas Déranger* printed in bold letters.

He had sent his pictures to a conservation site. Since there were no other flags nearby, it had to be the same one.

"I think it is."

She leaned against him. "I'm so glad that wasn't destroyed." She whispered the words into the night, the feeling behind them very clear.

She was amazing. After the day they'd had, the fact that she could be grateful for something so small…yet so important…

Dieu.

He turned her toward him and stared into her eyes, an overpowering urge coursing through him. Without stopping to think, he murmured, "I think I want to kiss you right now, Rach."

Her mouth turned up in a slight smile. "I think I'd like that, too."

Maybe the moonlit night was affecting his ability to make rational decisions, or maybe it was the lingering urgency from the day's events, but that was all it took. His head came down, and he took her lips with a fierceness that surprised him.

Maybe it had nothing at all to do with the moon or the day. Maybe it was the woman herself and the fact that he'd had a hard time working with her without thinking about that night a year ago. Had wanted to recreate it so many times. Was this the universe giving him permission?

Probably not. But how would this be any different from that night? It hadn't wrecked either of them, had it? They'd both moved forward with their lives, right?

His heart seemed to agree with his head for once as he deepened the kiss, using her body language as a guide for how much pressure to use and where she wanted it. His lips trailed down the side of her jaw, relishing the way she tilted her head to give him access to the areas he knew she liked.

The shoes she'd been carrying dropped to

the ground as she wrapped her arms around his neck.

Hell, if they were going to stop, they needed to do it now. His eyes caught sight of the nearest cabana, and it seemed to beckon to him, whispering for him to come inside. They had a choice to make. "Rachel."

"Mmm?" Her eyes looked up at him with a heat that matched what was running through his veins.

He nodded toward the nearest bungalow.

"Yes," she whispered.

That was all he needed. He swept her into his arms.

Rachel giggled. "My shoes…"

"Leave them for later."

She made no protest as he carried her to the dock and strode down it with her. The sign on the door read, Staff and Patients of Centre Hospitalier Only.

Well, they fit that description, right? He reached down and pulled the knob on the door, and it swung open without a sound. There was no one on the beach at this hour, and he could barely even see the hospital from here. Moving inside, he set her down, closing the door and leaning it against it. Then he hauled her against him.

The kiss changed from something hurried

and frantic to more leisurely. He wanted to slow things down. To do what Rachel had said and be willing to take the time needed—to pack those grounds tightly enough to make the end product good. So very good.

So he used tiny touches to kiss her mouth, her eyelids, the crook of her neck, his hands sliding beneath her shirt and pressing against the warm, bare skin of her back.

So silky. So soft. Just like she'd been the last time.

There was no bed in the hospital cabanas. Just a couple of hard wooden chairs. But they didn't need a bed this time. Didn't need anything except what was happening right now, here in the dark, quiet confines of this space. There were no stars to guide their path, since the front shutters that opened toward the ocean were shut tight. But he didn't need stars. Didn't need anything to guide him but instinct. Whether that was a good thing or bad, he didn't know. And he didn't really care right now.

Sweeping her shirt up and over her head, he held it in one hand for a few seconds, unsure what to do with it. Then she took it from him and threw it against the wall.

"It'll survive." She stood on tiptoe to reach his mouth.

It might survive, but would he?

She followed suit, unbuttoning his shirt and pushing it down his arms until it too fell away. Her fingers skated down his chest and reached the waistband of his jeans. He shuddered and grabbed her hand.

"Rach. Are you absolutely sure?"

She gave a low laugh. "Does it feel like I'm sure?"

It did. Oh, hell, it did.

He bent and swooped his arm under her ass and picked her up off her feet, walking to one of the chairs and lowering himself into it while her feet planted on the ground. His hands went to her hips, and with a grin, he inched her forward until her knees bumped against his, wordlessly asking her to make a decision.

She bent down and kissed him, hands on either side of his face, and then, just as he'd hoped she'd do, she straddled him, coming to rest tightly against him.

He groaned. "You're right about packing those grounds. It makes it. So. Much. Better." He punctuated each of those words with a kiss.

"I told you." She nipped his bottom lip hard enough to make part of him jerk against her.

Yes, she had. And right now, he believed her. Very much so.

He took her skirt, bunching it up in his hands,

finding it had a stretchy waist. "Will this slide over your head?"

"Why don't you try it and find out?"

Her tone said she already knew the answer to that question. So he slid it upward, taking his time, knuckles purposely lingering over the swell of her breasts. He paused there for a long minute before continuing on his way until her skirt was no more. Instead, this hot, fierce woman who sat astride him was dressed only in her bra and silky underwear. And when she did a little wiggle in his lap, he almost lost it.

"Not so fast," he muttered against her mouth.

His hands went to her waist, and he leaned forward to breathe in her scent, starting at her neck and moving to her collarbone, which he licked across. Then, using pressure from his palms, he tilted her back, farther and farther, until she was arched in just the perfect position.

Dieu, she looked wanton and so, so sexy with her hair tumbling behind her and her breasts jutting out for the taking.

And take he did, leaning forward to take one hard nipple into his mouth, sucking in a steady stream that made her gasp, her hands coming up and holding his mouth to her.

There was no need. He had no intention of leaving, using his teeth to hold her in place as his tongue swept over her again and again until he could stand it no longer.

With a growl, he reached behind her and undid her bra while she squirmed against him. The tiny garment fell away, and he buried his face in her breasts, sucking and kissing until he thought he was going to burst.

His breathing unsteady, he leaned back so he could get at his pocket to pull his wallet out. He took out the condom he'd carried ever since their first encounter and ripped it open.

Rachel seemed to sense his impatience, or maybe she was as impatient as he was, because she slid backward on his legs, fumbling with the button and zipper to his jeans, and then freed him, the warm air flowing around him in a tantalizing hint of what was to come. She wrapped her hand around him and held him there, her eyes finding his as her teeth bit into her lower lip. And then she pumped.

"*Mon Dieu, femme*, you're killing me."

"No. Not killing you. Just hoping to drive you to the brink."

If her hand wasn't already doing that, her words certainly did. He grabbed her to hold her still while he counted to ten in his head.

When he finally opened his eyes, there was this seductive, cunning smile on her face, as if she knew exactly how close he'd been. He leaned her closer so that his mouth was against her ear. "You are going to pay for that."

With that, he sheathed himself and tugged the elastic of her panties to one side, then he lifted her hips and set her down on top of him, thrusting up as he seated her fully onto him.

Tight—crazy tight—were the only words that came to mind as her heat and wetness squeezed at him. He had to hold her still yet again as he strained to control the urges that were telling him to lose himself in her. But *Dieu*, he wanted this to last. *Needed* it to last.

As soon as he could breathe again, he balled up a handful of hair, the silky locks trailing over his wrist, and leaned over her until she was lying back across his thighs. He shifted his hips forward and slid off the edge of the chair until his knees hit the ground, still buried inside her. He needed to be fully against her, to feel the scrape of his body against hers, so he laid them both down on the polished wooden planks.

"Okay?" he asked, looking at her face.

"Oui. C'est fantastique."

He smiled at her attempt at French, then responded in kind, a steady stream of words and phrases telling her how long he'd wanted to do this. What he wanted to do, how many times. And those times were as numerous as the stars they'd looked at when they stepped onto the beach. Her hand slid up his back and toyed with the hair at the back of his neck. And it felt so good. So damned good.

He began moving. Slow. Deep. Steady.

Rachel braced her feet on the ground, moving just ahead of him, forcing him to quicken his pace. As if she couldn't get enough. Her hips edged higher and higher with each thrust, taking him impossibly deep. She was tugging him toward a place he didn't want to go. Where the rising tide of desire became harder and harder to push back against. Harder to override. Harder to say no to.

"Seb... Seb..."

Her fingers dug into his back, and she arched into him, a sound coming from her throat. Then she suddenly pumped hard and fast against him, eyes closing as she went rigid.

Spasms rocked his world as he tried to somehow remain anchored to reality. But it was useless. Her orgasm shot him over the edge to his own climax as he thrust into her again and again.

Then it was over. His pace slowed, a sense of well-being and languorous satisfaction washing over him. He pulled in a breath and released all the stress from the last couple of days.

Rolling to his side, he drew her to him and

settled her against his chest, not willing to think about anything right now. Not the ramifications. Not the reality of what they'd just done. Not how it would affect their future dealings. All he wanted to do was sleep for a little while. Next to her. Inside her. And then he could deal with all the other stuff later.

Much later.

CHAPTER TEN

"BLEU..."

The sound of his voice woke her up. It was pitch-black, and she was disoriented for several minutes before realizing she was lying against something.

No. Against some*one*.

It was Seb. His head turned to one side, and he muttered again in his sleep, the words unintelligible, but the grief behind them caught at her heart. He was dreaming about his son.

Horror washed over her at catching him in such an intimate moment. Was that what had been behind him pulling her into his arms—missing his son? She didn't know, but she suddenly didn't want to be here anymore. Didn't want to know what his reasons were, because she was afraid his answer wouldn't be the one she wanted to hear.

Oh, God! She loved him!

She quickly but quietly scrambled to her feet,

her gaze going to him time and time again, and she wondered how she could have let this happen as she found her clothes and slipped them on. Fortunately, he didn't move, even when her toe accidentally slid her phone a few inches across the wooden floor and the screen lit up. Three o'clock. She could make it home and shower and then be at work again the next day looking completely normal. Unfazed by what had happened.

Except it would all be a lie. Inside she was a mess. A scared, crazy mess of conflicting emotions. What if he thought she expected something from him? Wanted them to be a family.

And she did. Dear God, she did. But she couldn't be a substitute for what he'd had with his own family. Couldn't risk getting involved with someone again so quickly. Just like she'd done with Roy. Look how that had turned out.

She and Seb had only really gotten to know each other over this last week. A week wasn't long enough. Hell, she doubted two years would be long enough to feel secure in a relationship. And then there was Claire…

Her daughter… Her eyes shut. She just couldn't risk it. Not yet.

Slipping from the cabana, she started to pad down the beach on silent feet before stopping. Could she really leave him in there naked?

What if he didn't wake up until morning and some unsuspecting fisherman came up on him?

She would call his phone as soon as she got to the boardwalk, when she was far enough away that he wouldn't see her. When he couldn't catch up with her. With that decided, and using the moon and stars to guide her way, she hurried down the beach. Just to the left was the sea turtle's nest, and she gave it a wide berth so it could remain undisturbed.

Please, please stay asleep, Seb. Just until I get farther away.

She had to get home. Home, where she could dissect everything that had happened and figure out where to go from there. One thing she did know was she could not sleep with him again. Not and maintain any semblance of professionalism. She loved him. And she didn't want him to know. Not yet. Maybe not ever.

The last time they were together like this, he'd recoiled from her after they'd woken up. She couldn't go through that again. Not with him. Not with anyone. It's why she couldn't wake him up before she left the cabana. Couldn't bear to see the look in his eyes if she stretched her hand out toward him.

For some men, it really was all about the sex. At least, that's what she'd heard. And God. *God!* She wished it could be that way for her, too. And it had been the time she'd been with a completely different man when Claire was younger. But from the first time she'd slept with Seb, there had been a weird sense of finality about it. As if he was going to be it for her.

And she didn't want him to be it. Not with all the baggage they both carried around with them.

By the time her feet hit the boardwalk, she was running. Running as fast as she could to her car, only then realizing her shoes were still somewhere on the beach where they'd left them.

But there was no way she was going back for them now. She'd do it tomorrow, in the daylight. When he was no longer in that cabana, waiting to look at her with eyes that told her to get the hell away from him.

Because she was so afraid that, just like Roy, he would run. As fast as he could.

Like she was doing right now?

No, that was different. She was running to keep from being hurt all over again. To keep Claire from being hurt. And no matter what it took, that's what she was going to do. Keep her daughter from paying the price for her stupidity. Even if doing that caused a pain she thought she'd never feel again.

Once seated in her car, she took a deep breath and tried to calm her nerves before dialing his number. She waited and waited until he finally answered. His voice was low. Sleepy. And so so sexy. How she wanted to go back. But she didn't. Instead, she quietly said she'd had to leave. And then she hung up the phone and put the vehicle into Reverse and drove away.

All he'd found were her shoes. Just like Cinderella. Only this was no fairy tale. This was reality.

Sebastien had woken up to his phone ringing and Rachel's voice saying she'd had to leave. No explanation. Just that. He came fully awake in a flash, realizing he wasn't in his bed. And he was completely alone.

He glanced at his phone. It was three thirty in the damn morning.

Things came back to him in a rush.

He and Rachel had spent the night at the cabana. At least, he had. How long ago had she left? Right afterward? She couldn't face him, so she just walked out?

By the time he'd dragged his clothes on and left the structure, he was angry, and he had no idea why. He trudged up the beach, spotting a pair of white shoes on the sand and realizing they were Rachel's. So she hadn't erased every sign of her presence.

He understood that it might be embarrassing to face him before leaving, but the least she could have done was say goodbye.

Like he'd done the last time they were together?

He'd been hell-bent on escape when she'd woken up and caught him and, probably not realizing that he was looking for a quick exit, had reached out to trace his tattoo. She hadn't gotten the chance to touch it this time. He'd made sure they were front to front the whole time they were together. Even as they fell asleep.

Had it been a move of self-preservation?

Maybe. Or maybe a way to control the intimacy level. To keep things from getting too personal. That was a more likely scenario. And looking at it now, it came across as selfish and cold. That woman had given everything she had, both at Mauhali and during their lovemaking. At the time, he thought he was, too. But looking back, he could see a sense of calculation behind keeping the focus on the physical and completely off the emotional.

Had she guessed?

He slid through the door at the hospital and into the elevator without attracting any attention. Things were normally pretty quiet this time of night. He made it to his office. Plunked her shoes onto his desk and then sank onto his couch for a few minutes to try to pull himself together.

The anger was gone, dissipated during that walk of shame down the beach. None of this was her fault.

Rachel was probably already home, fast asleep in her bed. Hopefully they could both put this behind them and go about their professional lives without any problems. Without any complications.

Without any…

That tiny flicker of fear came out of nowhere, just like it had the last time they'd been together. He'd forgotten about it until this very second, when it hit him full force again.

He and Layla had used a condom, too.

And something had gone wrong. She'd wound up pregnant. At the time, he'd been over the moon. He'd always wanted to be a father. He'd leaped at the chance to propose to her. Layla had wanted to put the wedding off until after she'd had the baby and lost the baby weight. He'd been fine with all of it.

Until something worse than a condom failure had gone wrong after Bleu's birth and his baby had been diagnosed with cancer.

What if it happened again?

What if there was something in his DNA

that was defective…that had caused Bleu's cancer? That could cause it again if he ever made someone pregnant? The oncologist at the time had brushed off his concerns, saying it wasn't possible. But how much did they really know about genetic code?

This wasn't just about Sebastien and his fears, though. There was a lot more at stake than that.

There was Rachel. She'd already gone through cancer with one child—was he willing to risk it happening again, all because he couldn't control his impulses?

What if it was already too late?

The likelihood of two condom failures for the same man was probably pretty remote. But once the thought had taken hold, it was becoming impossible to shake.

He got up from the couch and grabbed a set of clothes, going into his tiny office bathroom and stepping under a blast of brutally cold water. Flagellating himself for what he couldn't take back?

He stood there for as long as he could stand it and then soaped himself up and rinsed before turning off the tap.

Drying himself, he slicked back his hair and dressed in his fresh set of clothes, stuffing the ones from last night into a plastic bag. He could do those when he got home.

He went back into his office and then clicked open the screen of his laptop to see a set of headlines in bold letters across the top of his screen: Tropical Cyclone Koji Is No More.

Except it was. Because in its aftermath, it had caused some changes that no one could have predicted. Not even him. Because somewhere amid those strewn mangoes and fallen trees, something else had fallen.

His heart.

Was that why he'd been so focused on the physical part of lovemaking—because he hadn't wanted to recognize the truth?

Merde. He repeated the epithet over and over in his head until the word came out in an audible growl.

How could this have happened?

How could he have *let* this happen?

He lay down on his couch to get a couple of hours of sleep. And he must have, because the sudden sound of knocking dragged him to his feet. He scrambled to find his senses. Hell, that was probably her, and he had no idea what he was going to say to her this morning. Or any other morning, for that matter.

He strode to the desk and picked her shoes off the desk, dropping them to the floor behind it before he moved to the chair and sat down. He pushed the shoes under his desk with one foot.

Just in case it isn't her.

He was a liar. He just didn't want to have to hand them to her and acknowledge what had happened last night. Although maybe her leaving the way she had meant that she had no more desire to start a relationship than he did.

He might love her. But that didn't mean he should be with her. Or with anyone.

"Come in."

He schooled his features to look as impassive as possible.

The door opened, and a woman stood there. Except it wasn't Rachel. It was someone who looked vaguely familiar, but...

Then a little girl stepped out from behind her, and it hit him. It was Sharon, the drowning victim, and her mom. Man, it seemed like eons ago that he and Rachel had spent time on the beach under completely different circumstances.

He stood in a rush and ushered them into his office.

Marie smiled at him. "Sharon wanted to come by today. She couldn't wait." She nudged the girl deeper into the office. "Go ahead. Give it to him."

The child stepped forward, holding two envelopes in her hand. "This is for you." She held one out to him.

He smiled and knelt in front of her. "For me? Thank you." He glanced at the manila envelope. "Can I open it?"

She nodded.

Seb stuck a finger under the glued flap and coaxed it free. Then he slid the single item from inside and turned it over to face him.

His smile was still firmly affixed, but a lump formed in his throat. He vaguely remembered Marie wanting to take a picture of him, Sharon and Rachel right before she was discharged from the hospital. In the photo they were all smiling. All totally happy with the miraculous outcome. And Sebastien had been totally unaware of what was to come less than a week later.

Right now there was no miraculous outcome in sight.

"Thank you for this. I like it a lot," he said to Sharon.

Sharon gave him the biggest smile ever, one front tooth missing. "Can you give this one to the lady doctor?"

Seb glanced up at the child's mother who nodded. "We asked for her at the nurses' desk in the emergency room, but they sent up us here, and the people here said she hadn't arrived yet this morning."

"And I have to go to school."

The last thing he wanted to do was hand Rachel a picture of the two of them, even if there was a child separating them. Maybe having a child in the shot was even worse…it teased at something he felt he could never have again.

But he wasn't going to tell Sharon any of that. All she wanted to know was if he would see that Rachel got it. "I'll make sure she gets it." Even if that meant having it put in her staff mailbox.

He climbed to his feet and gave Marie another smile. "Thanks for coming in, and I'm really glad Sharon is doing so well."

"Yes, and we're glad the storm has gone."

"I think we all are." He held out his hand to Sharon and gave hers a gentle shake. "Enjoy your day at school."

With a last goodbye, they left his office.

He put Rachel's envelope on one of his end tables after he'd scrabbled under his desk to retrieve her shoes and made a mental note to do something about them. As for his own picture, he stuffed it back in the envelope before fishing it out again. He glanced over at his wall of kids, where he posted all the pictures sent to him by families of patients. If they ever came back again, they might question why their picture wasn't on his wall with all the others. So he retrieved a thumbtack from his desk drawer and stuck the picture on the wall, tempted to put another picture in front of Rachel to keep him from staring at her, before deciding that was immature and cowardly.

Like he was being about giving her the other snapshot?

He was going to see her in the flesh, day in and day out, unless she decided to take Philippe up on his offer. The last thing he wanted, though, was to be the reason she felt she needed to transfer out of the department.

Whether he wanted to or not, he needed to talk to her face-to-face and decide how to avoid something like last night happening again.

He would do it as soon as she came in.

Right on cue, Rachel popped her head around the door. "Can you come out and see a patient?"

She looked totally calm, totally relaxed. There was no sign that she was upset about anything. But he still needed to do the right thing.

"Sure. Is it an emergency?"

"Not exactly, but he's not happy. He has a fishhook stuck in his hand. He wouldn't let the ER doctors near him."

Even as she said it, he heard the sound of wailing coming from down the hall.

So much for hoping he could have a quick word with her before he went down to see the patient. It would have to wait until afterward.

"Let's go."

"Um…actually, Stella is down there with him. They're waiting on you. Hope that's okay."

In other words, she wasn't going to work with him on this case. Instead it would be a different nurse. "Yep. It's fine."

It was a lie, but what else was he going to say?

He got up from behind his desk, the shoes and envelope on the end table catching his eye. Now was not the time.

Making his way toward to the sounds of distress, he gave a quick knock before entering the room.

Inside, he found a patient he knew well, sitting on the exam table holding one hand in his lap. And, yep, there was a large fishing hook embedded in the flesh of his palm. The wailing stopped when he saw Seb. Maybe seeing a familiar face helped. "Looks like you caught yourself, Jacque, instead of a fish."

The boy's dad was sitting in one of the chairs. "Well, um, part of it might have been my fault."

Stella gave them both a smile. "This isn't the first fishing accident we've had up here."

"I didn't realize he was behind me getting a drink out of the cooler. And I went to cast my line…"

And he'd hooked his son.

"We'll get you all fixed up and on your way. You might even have time enough to do a little more fishing."

By the time Sebastien had taken the hook out of Jacque's hand and checked the date of his last tetanus vaccine, an hour had gone by.

The rest of the day went just like that case, with other nurses doing the workups and being there for the exams. He didn't work with Rachel once.

There was no way that was just coincidence. Which meant no matter how she'd looked when she came to get him this morning, she was upset about what had happened. She couldn't even stand being in the same room with him, evidently.

He didn't want to leave things this way. Didn't want her to feel so uncomfortable in his presence that she felt avoiding him was her only way out. Not only did he not want to cause anyone that kind of discomfort, he didn't want the other nurses to notice and wonder what was going on.

Because they *would* figure it out.

Picking up his phone, he dialed her number. Four rings went by, and just when he thought it was going to go to voice mail, she picked up. "Hello?"

"Hey, Rach. Can we meet somewhere to talk?"

"About?"

Despite himself, he couldn't help but smile. His communication skills obviously left something to be desired. At least with this particular woman.

"I think you might have some idea."

"I'm off in an hour. Can we meet in the courtyard area?"

"I'll see you there."

An hour later, he made his way to the courtyard, her shoes in a bag. She was already there, sitting on a bench in a more secluded corner away from those who were eating at the tables that were scattered throughout the space.

She sat straighter when she spotted him coming toward her, hands clasped tightly in her lap.

He set the bag beside her, wishing he'd brought her coffee as well. She tilted her head before peering inside. Her eyes widened. "Oh! My shoes. Thanks for bringing them back. I didn't realize they were missing until I got back to the parking lot."

"Not a problem." He hesitated and then motioned her to a seat. "You could have woken me, you know, instead of sneaking away and calling me on the phone."

"I didn't sneak away…" She gave him a sheepish look. "Okay, I might have, but I just wasn't sure what to say. I don't think either of us meant for that to happen. And I have Claire to think about. It's been just her and me for a very long time."

"Her dad?"

"He's been out of the picture since she was an infant. He just one day decided he wasn't cut out to be a father. And that was that."

His jaw tightened. Wasn't that the exact thing he'd decided? That he didn't want to be a father? But hell, he would have never walked out on Bleu. Not ever. "I'm sorry, Rachel. I didn't know."

"So you see why I don't want to be involved with anyone right now. Not even to…" She gave a shrug.

He assumed she was talking about sex.

He'd come here, expecting to be the bad guy and tell her that what happened couldn't happen again, but it looked like she was beating him to the punch. Letting him off the hook, the same way he'd plucked that fishhook from young Jacque's hand.

He decided to be up-front with her, even though it was one of the hardest things he'd ever done. "I'm sorry you had to go through that. Bleu was the result of a failed condom, but I loved him more than anything. When he died, I decided I couldn't face being a father again. And even though I know the odds of another condom failing are astronomical… I still think about it. So you don't have to worry about anything happening again."

"Is it going to be too awkward working together? There's that position in Orthopedics, and after going to Mauhali, I've been thinking it might be a good fit for me."

Was it going to be too awkward? They'd survived the awkwardness last time, so something didn't ring quite true. Was there more to it than that?

"With Dr. Chauvre. Yes, I remember. Pediatrics would hate to lose you. You're good with your patients, and I'd hoped you like being here as well."

Okay, so now he was sounding like a boss, which hadn't been his intent. But he didn't want her leaving because of him.

"Yes. I do like it here. I just have a lot to think about. And Claire—"

Her phone buzzed, and they both froze for a second before she looked down at the instrument in her hand. She stared at it as it rang a second time, then she closed her eyes for a second and stood. "I need to go answer this."

She gave a visible swallow. "And just so you know. You don't have to worry about last night ever happening again. I've taken care of that."

With that, she walked away, answering her phone. The last thing he heard her say was, "Hi, honey," before she was out of earshot, leaving him sitting alone. Alone with his thoughts. Alone with her shoes. Alone with his future.

A future that suddenly stretched before him like a vast wasteland.

CHAPTER ELEVEN

HER FLIGHT HOME was a whole lot harder than she'd thought it would be. Claire had called as she was talking to Seb, and all of a sudden she knew she needed to go be with her daughter. He'd said *Pediatrics* would hate to lose her and listed some reasons, but none of them had to do with him. He'd never said *he'd* hate to lose her. That had been a blow, even though her reasons for thinking about Orthopedics had been true, that she thought it might be a good fit for her.

And with his confession that he never wanted to be a father again, she'd heard a second nail hitting the coffin of hope. With his fear about being caught in the circumstances surrounding his son's birth, she realized she didn't have the stomach to work with him day in and day out. Not anymore. Not after that last night together and knowing there was no hope that he might return her feelings. Not that she wanted him to. She'd told him the truth. Claire had to be her first priority. Especially knowing how he felt about fatherhood.

So she'd booked a flight, leaving a few hours after her talk with Seb. Because every time she thought about what they'd done on that beach, it left her shaky and out of sorts. The last thing she wanted was for him to guess. And if she saw him before she could sort out her thoughts, he would see it written across her face. That she loved him. That she wanted to be with him again. Far too much. Having him tuck her against him had felt more right than anything had in years. And the way Claire had hit it off with him would make it harder.

So much harder.

She'd already gotten matchmaker vibes from her daughter. As if she might like to see the two of them together.

Sorry, baby, he doesn't want it. And I don't want you hurt.

She stared out the window of the plane as it started its descent into Wisconsin. Taurati was already a long way behind her, and so was Sebastien. The hospital administrator had been great when she'd said she needed some personal time. He'd acted like it was a simple case of burnout after putting in so much overtime. But it was so much more than that.

And somehow she had to face Claire and

her mom and act like everything was fine. She somehow had to pretend that a lightning bolt hadn't hit her on her walk back from that cabana, when she'd realized she loved him.

She'd stupidly done what she warned herself not to do for years. In fact she'd shrugged off men, telling herself she'd have plenty of time for that once Claire was grown and gone.

But for it to happen now? *Now?*

How had she let this happen?

And what was she going to do about it? The easiest thing would be to stay in the States. But Claire would not believe that her mom had simply decided she missed her home country enough to quit her job and fly home. And it wasn't fair to her daughter not to let her have a say in the decision. Claire loved Taurati. It was as if she'd finally been able to put her diagnosis behind her and start living.

They both had.

And to backtrack on all that?

She didn't know. So she was going to take a week. Maybe two. And she was going to do some soul searching and try to make some sense out of all that had happened.

The wheels hit the runway, and the sensation of air brakes engaging was unmistakable. It was as if the whole plane gave a collective sigh of relief. Not that it had been a rough flight in the sense of turbulence or anything. Nothing like that helicopter ride to Mauhali. In fact, if anything, the weather had been silky smooth on each leg of her journey. Except for in the pit of her stomach, where a mini cyclone was busy whirling her insides into a mess of self-doubt and fear.

Just enjoy Claire. That is all you have to do right now.

Sebastien and Taurati could wait for a couple of days. In fact, if they had to, they could wait forever.

The plane finished docking at the gate, and the doors opened. Rachel gathered her belongings and started wheeling her carry-on down the narrow aisle. She hadn't checked any baggage. She'd fled with just a few possessions. If it came down to it, and she decided to leave the hospital, she could have a moving company pack up her apartment and ship her stuff to her.

She would never have to face Seb again if she didn't want to. One thing she knew, though. She was never going to forget him. Not for as long as she lived. It would take her heart a long, long time to get over him.

Entering the airport terminal, her eyes sought out and found her loved ones within seconds. Claire raced toward her and caught her in a fierce hug. "I'm so glad you're here.

Grams said the storm died out and that no one died on that other island."

"It did." Her next words were chosen with care. "Taurati was very lucky."

It may have been. But she didn't think she'd come out quite as unscathed as they had.

Her mom reached her and put her hands on her shoulders, studying her. "Welcome home, honey."

"Thanks, Mom." Rachel's smile felt brittle and so very fake. Because this didn't seem like home. Not anymore. She wasn't sure there was any place on earth that felt like that right now.

Except for Taurati. And she didn't know if she could face going back there.

"How is Sebastien?" asked Claire. "Does he miss me?"

The question slashed her heart in two. She'd tried to prevent her daughter from becoming attached to the man. To any man. But in the end, could you really choose whom you loved?

"He's fine. I'm sure he's really tired from all the work he put in on the cyclone and the rescue efforts on the other island. Everyone's relieved that they didn't have to evacuate the hospital."

Ugh! She'd left her shoes beside Seb on the bench. She'd been so intent on getting out of there that she'd totally forgotten about them until now. If she didn't go back, she assumed he'd toss them in the trash.

Actually he'd probably toss a lot more than just her shoes. In the end, she'd saved him from having to let her down easy. The last time he'd run. This time it was her.

And damn, she'd thought it would feel a whole lot more empowering than it did. As it was, it just seemed…cowardly.

She should have stayed. Should have been truthful about how she felt and then made her decision based on his reaction. And she might have, if he hadn't talked about not wanting to be a father. To her, that was his decision.

Maybe if she'd been more careful with her heart…

But she hadn't been.

She dropped a kiss on her daughter's head, realizing she wouldn't be able to do that much longer. Her daughter had grown over the last year. And not just physically. She'd grown in confidence and knowledge. How could she tell her they might not be going back to Taurati?

She wouldn't. Not yet. Not until she decided what to do about the island and about Sebastien.

"Can we call him? He promised to help me with my French and Tahitian."

"Let's hold off on that for a while. I'm sure

Seb needs some time to unwind after the crazy week we've had."

Had it only been a week? It had.

A week to fall in love. The words sounded like they belonged on the cover of a romance novel. But this novel's ending? Uncertain at best.

She decided to distract Claire as they headed for the parking garage. "Guess what I saw a couple of days ago?"

"What?"

"I was walking on the beach and saw a flag where that sea turtle laid her eggs."

"Oh, wow. You're sure it was the same spot?"

"Yes. It was nighttime, so it was dark, but the moon was shining and we… I mean, *I* know it was the right spot."

"I wish I could have seen it. I miss Taurati."

"I know you do."

Rachel's heart ached as she reached for her daughter's hand and held it tight as her mom motioned toward one of the rows of cars.

"Speaking of sea turtles, I put the one Sebastien gave me on a shelf in Grams's house. I can't wait to get it back to our apartment on Taurati and put it in my room."

She swallowed past a lump in her throat. "I can't wait for that, either. But for right now, let's just enjoy Grams and Gramps and being all together, okay?"

"Okay."

And with that, they reached the car and the conversation turned to what had happened in Wisconsin since Claire had arrived. Rachel settled in the front seat and leaned her head against the headrest and listened to her daughter, all the while trying not to break down in front of them. That could come later. When she was all alone, and no one could see her cry.

Neves Bouchet paid Sebastien a visit two days after his conversation with Rachel.

"To what do I owe this sudden appearance?" he asked the man as he settled onto the couch in his office.

"I just wanted to thank you for all your and Rachel's hard work on the hospital's behalf. And for going to Mauhali to help with the rescue attempts. I'll admit, it's the first time I've ever been glad for hospital plans to have been abandoned midstream. But at least Mauhali benefited from them. I hear that your flail chest patient is doing well after surgery to stabilize her ribs."

"Yes, I heard that as well." Out of the corner of his eye, he caught sight of his end table. Hell! The shoes Rachel had left behind again were there in plain sight. He'd taken them out of the bag and then totally forgotten about them. But to get up and move them now would just draw attention to them.

Hopefully Neves hadn't noticed.

"I wanted to thank Rachel in person, but she decided to take some personal days, saying she wanted to go see her mom and daughter. I assume she'll be bringing her daughter back with her?"

The question slid past him as he processed what the man had just said. Rachel was in Wisconsin? He'd been so relieved not to run into her yesterday that it had never dawned on him that it might be because she wasn't here at the hospital. Or on Taurati. He'd assumed that it was her day off.

"I'm not sure. I didn't realize she was gone."

"She didn't tell you she was leaving?"

Merde. No, she hadn't. Was it because of their conversation?

He swallowed as another thought hit him. Was it permanent?

"Actually, she didn't. When did she ask for the time off?"

"Day before yesterday."

The day of their talk. There was no way that could be a coincidence. His mind ran through everything he'd said, trying to figure out what could have made her suddenly decide to leave. He thought they'd been in agreement on everything.

"Did she say when she'd be back?"

"She said she needed at least a week. Maybe two."

Or maybe she needed forever. Maybe she'd never be back.

His chest tightened as a thousand emotions went through him. If he'd known, would that conversation have ended differently?

"I didn't know."

"Yes, you said that." Neves fixed him with a look. "Is there anything *I* should know?"

The man's head turned toward the end table, and he caught sight of the shoes before his gaze swiveled back to Seb.

So much for hoping Neves wouldn't notice. Truthfully, not much got past his friend. It was what made him such a good hospital administrator. And such a great judge of character.

And he'd pegged exactly what might have happened.

"I think you've already guessed. I'm just not sure what to do about it."

"I take it it's complicated. Not like Laurence and Britan?"

"Nothing like that."

The other couple had followed the normal

trajectory of romance—One: Noticing each other. Two: Going on the usual number of dates. Three: A proposal followed by marriage.

"Okay, I'm taking off my hospital administrator hat and putting on my friend cap. Do you care about her, Seb?"

This time he looked the man in the eye. "I do." The answer was simple. So simple that it seemed ludicrous when he said it aloud. It was that simple. And that complicated.

Because he wasn't sure he could do the whole family thing again. Sometimes love just wasn't enough. And after hearing about Rachel's ex taking off because he couldn't handle being a father? Well, he wasn't going to pursue Rachel unless he knew beyond a shadow of a doubt that he could handle the fears and ramifications of what a decision like that might entail.

"Then you've got a decision to make, haven't you? And I suggest you figure it out, Seb. If you don't even try…" His friend stood and glanced again at the shoes. " Well, you'll regret it more than you know." With a smile to soften the words, he headed for the door.

Figure it out. Easy words to say. Not so easy to do.

But Neves was right. If he just continued to coast through life, he could very well miss out on something good. Something beautiful.

Like having a family?

The door clicked behind his friend, and Sebastien shook his head and then tried to bury himself in his work.

CHAPTER TWELVE

IT HAD BEEN a week.

And there was still no sign of Rachel. Neves said he hadn't heard from her, either.

The hospital administrator had told him, "Figure it out, Seb. Or I think you'll regret it more than you know."

Would he? Hell, yes, he would.

He'd been so sure he couldn't be a father again after Bleu. Had been steadfast in that commitment. Then along came Rachel and her daughter, making him doubt everything in his life.

Hell, he loved her. Loved her for her fierce determination to do the right thing for herself and for Claire. To do the right thing for her patients.

But could he let his heart rule and forge a life with someone whose daughter could relapse in the future? After six years, it was unlikely but not impossible. Just like cyclones on Taurati.

But even if she felt the same way, what if Rachel wanted more children? The neurosurgeon years ago had told him that neuro cancers were rarely caused by genes that were passed down. The key word being *rarely*.

Could he take the chance that the doctor he'd despised all those years ago was actually right?

It was either that or let life go on the way it was now. Let Rachel make her decision to stay in Wisconsin or come back with no interference from him. He'd done that for a week. Had sat back and let nature take its course.

And he'd been the most miserable *enfoiré* the hospital had ever seen. He didn't see that changing anytime soon, if he didn't take Neves's advice.

He'd told her he hadn't wanted children, right after she'd talked about her ex walking out on her. He could well imagine what had gone through her head. That if she opened her heart to him, it could very well happen all over again.

What she didn't know was that if he made the decision to be in her life, he wouldn't go back on it, which was one of the reasons that decision was so damned hard to make.

Make it. Just make it. And then tell her.

She might not believe him…might tell him to shove off, but all he was responsible for were his own actions.

And his own inactions.

A cyclone of a different type hit his heart. Neves was right. He didn't have to sit back and passively watch something wither away, the way he'd been forced to do with his son. This time he actually had the power to do something about it. If he was willing to try.

If Rachel was willing to let him try.

He went over and picked up one of her shoes, turning it over in his hands before setting it down with a sense of fierce resolution. Yes. He was willing.

It was a terrifying prospect, but then again, falling in love with her had been just as terrifying. But it could also be something beautiful. He'd seen that during their time in Mauhali. During the night in that cabana.

If he was willing to get off his ass and go after it. He had no idea what kind of reception he'd be met with. But that didn't matter. What did matter was that he made the effort. That he was willing to be honest with her. And with himself.

To find out if she was willing to risk everything—just as he was—in order to become a family. And yes, he wanted it. Like he'd never wanted anything.

He called Neves. The man picked up on the first ring, as if he'd been waiting for the call, barking into the phone, "Did you figure it out yet?"

Seb laughed. "How did you know?"

"I couldn't imagine any other reason you'd be calling me. Or at least, I'd hoped not. So what's the plan?"

"Hell, I have no idea." Sebastien realized it was true. But he was done sitting at his desk mooning after what he'd let slip through his fingers. "But I need some time off."

"You've got it."

"Don't you want to know how much?"

"Nope." His friend paused. "All I care about is that you both find what you are looking for. For all our sakes."

"Why can't I call him?"

Claire's requests had gotten more and more insistent, and Rachel was running out of plausible excuses. She hadn't heard from Sebastien since she'd left.

But had she really expected to?

No. But it hurt that he could just let her leave without doing anything to stop her.

Had she tried to stop Roy when he left? No. She'd just kind of given him a mental good-riddance boot, and then she'd had to work through so many layers of anger and despair afterward.

She bit her lip. Hadn't she done the exact

same thing Roy had done—run from a situation that she didn't think she could deal with?

Why would she expect Sebastien to react any differently than she had when faced with someone wanting out of her life?

Except she didn't really want him out of her life. Much to the contrary. But she was scared. Scared it wouldn't work out. Scared that she and Claire were both going to be hurt if he rejected them. Scared that Sebastien's fear of becoming father again was something he couldn't get past. And she knew that's what it was. A fear of loss. It was the same thing that had led her to reject him.

So she'd left Taurati before he got the chance to hurt her and Claire.

But she'd also left before either of them had had time to fully process what had happened in the beach cabana. Things between them had changed so fast that she hadn't thought straight that day in the courtyard. He hadn't rejected her, though. She'd been the one to initially say that what had happened would never happen again.

Claire had been the only thing on her mind. But her daughter liked him. Even if things didn't work out romantically between them, she trusted Seb enough to know he wouldn't reject her daughter.

His offer of help with her French and Tahitian? It wouldn't be withdrawn. If she'd learned anything about Sebastien over the last year of working with him, it was that he kept his word whenever possible.

He'd lost his son in a horrible, devastating way. From what he'd said, he was just as scared as she was. Maybe even more so. He'd as much as said that loss weighed on his mind when he was with someone.

Didn't Roy's behavior weigh on hers when she thought about falling in love? Yes, it did.

She looked at her daughter, who was waiting expectantly for her answer. Then she sucked down a deep breath and decided to risk it all. For love.

And for Claire.

"There's no reason why you can't. Go ahead."

Swallowing hard, she watched her daughter punch the number in.

Please, Seb, don't hurt her. God...don't hurt her.

"Sebastien? It's Claire! How are you?"

Her daughter's face was animated, her smile wide as she listened to whatever he was saying. "I miss Taurati a lot, but I'm keeping up with my French studies. I still need help with Tahitian, though."

Her eyes widened. "You're where?"

Rachel's heart tightened. Had he left Taurati, like she had?

Her daughter pulled the phone down from her ear. "Mom, he's here! Sebastien is here."

"What? Where?" Her heart began pounding out of her chest.

"He's in Wisconsin. He wants to talk to you." Claire held the phone out to her.

Seb was in Wisconsin? Was there some kind of symposium?

No, that was ridiculous. He wouldn't come all the way here for that.

Then for what?

A ripple of hope went through her, starting at the outer reaches of her limbs and moving with ever-increasing speed toward her heart. Nails that had been pounded in during their last meeting started losing their hold.

She took the phone with a hand that shook. "Seb?"

"Hi."

That one simple word filled her with a warmth that made her relax into the couch. "Hi yourself. Claire said you're in Wisconsin? What in the world?"

"I am here. I was getting ready to call you, but Claire beat me to it."

He really was in her home state. But she still had no idea why. "What part of Wisconsin?"

"Your part. Black River Falls."

Her lips parted. She'd been imagining Madison or Milwaukee. So no symposium. Which meant he was here for...

"A-are you staying in a hotel?"

"Not yet, but that's not what I want to talk about. Can we meet?"

Very aware that Claire was watching her with an expectancy that made her heart burn, she tried to think this through. She didn't want to talk here at her mom's house, just in case this wasn't the kind of meeting she was envisioning. The kind she was hoping for. Maybe he'd been sent to tell her her services were no longer required at the center.

That was ridiculous. They wouldn't have sent Seb here for that.

Which brought her back to that other reason that was tickling at the edges of her mind.

"Can you get to the library?"

"I can. I've rented a car, so I can meet you there."

"I'll see you in thirty minutes?" In truth, it would only take her about ten minutes to get to that particular place, but she needed a few minutes to gather her wits and figure out what she was going to say to him.

Tell him you love him.

"See you then."

The second she disconnected the call, Claire was all over it. "I want to come! Please, Mom, *please*!"

This was the hard part. There was no way she could tell Claire what had happened between them, or what she hoped might happen now, just in case she was wrong. "Not this time, honey. Seb and I need to talk. But if he's here for longer than just today, maybe we can work something out."

Claire's eyes went wide again. "What the... Do you love Seb or something?"

One thing she'd promised she would never do was lie to her daughter, if she could help it, so she simply nodded before adding, "But I'm not sure we can work it out. We're just going to talk, so don't get your hopes up."

As if she hadn't heard a thing Rachel had said, Claire flung her arms around her and clung to her for a minute. "You're going to tell him, aren't you?"

"It depends on why he's here." She stood, dislodging Claire, before kissing her on the cheek. "But now I need to go get ready."

She stopped and looked at her daughter. "No matter what happens, I want you to know that Sebastien is a good person. He and I have to do what's right for us. And what's right for you."

"I already know he's a good person. And I

promise not to be mad at him—or you—if you don't get together."

"Good to know, kiddo. Good to know." She dropped one last kiss on her cheek before sprinting to the bathroom to brush her hair.

She arrived at the library just on time and exited the car, pulling the hood of her down parka up around her face as she headed toward the entrance. She saw him before she was even halfway there. Rather than waiting inside the warm building, he was standing outside, in a simple gray sweat jacket. His hair was shorter than it had been when she was in Taurati.

"Why aren't you inside?" she said when she reached him.

"It's a little colder here than where I'm from." His nose was red, hands dug deep into the pockets of his jeans.

"Yes, it is. Come on. There's a coffee shop a few doors down. Let's go in there."

She still had no idea why he was here, but he looked so out of place in her environment. She smiled. Probably about as out of place as she looked in Taurati at times. But she loved it there. Missed the heat and the beach…and him.

They made it to the nearly empty coffee shop, and she pointed to table tucked away in the back, but first they had to order. "Have you eaten? They have some sandwiches, if you want something."

"I don't. Just some coffee."

Rachel glanced up at the menu, where the choices were mind-boggling for such a small town. "Do you have a preference?"

"I've taken a liking for your espressos. With sugar."

"Why don't you go get that table in the back, and I'll bring the coffees?"

When he nodded, she went up to the counter and ordered for them, waiting while their drinks were being prepared. She glanced toward the back, where Seb sat. He was blowing into his hands in a way that made her smile. He really was an island boy.

And she was a small-town girl. But somehow, together, they'd made a kind of magic that she doubted she'd ever experience with anyone else.

She was going to tell him. She couldn't let him leave without knowing. But first she needed to tell him why she'd left.

She got the cups and then headed for the table, setting his espresso in front of him. "One sweet espresso."

"Thanks." He took a sip.

God, she loved looking at him. Loved that

he was here, in her world. But she needed to know. "Why are you here, Seb?"

He set his coffee down and shrugged out of his jacket. "Isn't it obvious?"

"Maybe. I don't know." She bit her lip.

He sighed. "What happened— I've gone over and over the whys of that cabana, but I'm still not sure why you left Taurati so suddenly. Without any explanation. Did I do something?"

She needed to tell him. But she had no idea how. Maybe she could go back in time and help him understand.

"Remember when I told you about Claire's biological father?"

"Yes." He frowned. "Is he here? Is that why you came back?"

She blinked. "No. No, of course not. As far as I know, he'll never be back. But when you said you'd decided you didn't want to be a father again…"

Seb seemed to pale in front of her, and a few seconds went by before he replied. "You were afraid I might do the same thing? Leave?"

Something squirmed inside her. Did he feel the same way? "Are you saying you wouldn't?"

If that was the case, she wasn't sure why he'd made the trek halfway across the globe to find her.

"What I said was true. For a long time, I

didn't want to be a father, because of Bleu. I didn't think I had it in me to lose another child." He swallowed. "And I knew Claire had had cancer. It brought back so many memories. So many fears. And then I got to know her. And you."

"And now?"

"Over the last couple of days, I've come to realize that life can't be shoved into a neat package and be expected to stay there."

She smiled. She'd thought much the same thing. "I've been protective of Claire for a long time because of what she went through. And because of what her father did. I haven't wanted to see her get hurt. Especially by my dating anyone. I told myself my love life could wait until Claire was all grown-up." Time to lay it on the line. "And then you came along. But I also watched you fall all over yourself to get away from me that first time we were together. And so when we were together at the beach that last time, I left before you were awake because I was so afraid…"

His eyes closed, a muscle working in his cheek. "You were afraid I would run again. Like Claire's father. And hurt her. Hurt you."

All she could do was nod.

"I was afraid, too, Rach. Afraid I couldn't commit. Afraid I wasn't cut out to be a father."

He said all that as if it was in the past. Did that mean…?

"You're not afraid anymore?"

"I am *pétrifié*. You can't imagine how much. But I've decided the risk is worth it. You're worth it. And if I say I'll stay, you can believe it." He reached for her hand. "I love you. I think I have since that very first time we were together. I just couldn't admit it, even to myself. But I don't know how you feel about me. Or whether or not Claire could accept having me in your life."

A sudden rush of joy filled her heart. "So you mean—?"

"I want you in my life, Rachel. If you trust me. I promise I won't run. No matter how hard things get."

"This time I was the one who ran. And I'm sorry. I promise it's the last time. Because I love you, too."

"Dieu miséricordieux." His fingers tightened around her hand. "And Claire?"

"Claire has done nothing but talk about you ever since I got back. I had no idea how I was going to break it to her if we couldn't go back to Taurati. But she says she trusts us both."

"So this means you'll come back to the island with me? I'd be willing to stay here, but I'm not so sure I can survive the winters."

She laughed. "I'm not so sure you could, either."

"But I'd be willing to try, if that's what you wanted." Seb's palm slid behind her nape, and he met her halfway across the table, kissing her softly. "*Je t'aime*, Rachel Palmer."

As it always did, hearing her name murmured in those husky French tones made her shiver. "I love you, too."

There was another kiss, and when they parted, he murmured. "By the way, I brought your shoes."

The words were so unexpected, they made her laugh all over again. "To hell with my shoes. I'm just glad you brought you."

"You are, are you?"

She smiled and touched his hand. "I am. So, *so* glad."

They came together again, this kiss holding the promise of an enduring love and the happiness of a lifetime.

EPILOGUE

Two months later

SEB SAID HE wanted to take his time, using her own words against her, saying that the effort they put into their relationship now would make things even better. Any worry that he might back out and break Claire's heart, he kissed away whenever they could manage to find time together.

This time it was she who was impatient. But they'd worked through so much of their pasts. Together. Going step by step, telling each other their fears.

She'd told him hers—that she was afraid he might walk away from them like Roy had. He'd promised her he was here to stay. And she believed him.

And he'd told her how afraid he was of losing another child, how gutted and lost he'd been after Bleu had died. But despite that, he was willing to open his heart and love again. And Claire already loved him to pieces. They hadn't yet officially told her that they were together, but she knew. She just let them go on pretending she didn't. And Rachel loved her for that.

The doorbell to her apartment rang. Frowning, she went to answer it, thinking it might be one of Claire's friends, until she opened the door.

Seb stood there in shorts and flip-flops.

"Hi. I wasn't expecting you—or did I forget something?"

"No, but I have a surprise for you. Can you come?"

"Claire isn't home right now. Is this something she needs to be in on?"

He grinned. "Yes, but not right this second. I want you to see something. It'll take a couple of hours."

"So if you're in casual clothes, I'm assuming I can come as I am?" She glanced down at her gauzy skirt and T-shirt.

"You're perfect. We'll be in the sand, so bring shoes you can easily kick off."

Okay, she had no idea what he needed her to see at the beach, but she did as he said, sliding her feet into the easy-off sandals she'd worn the time they'd made love, and then grabbed her purse. "I'll text Claire on the way and let her know where I am."

Once in the car, he headed in the direction of the hospital, which was strange. He'd said they were going to be on the beach. So maybe it was the one out there.

He parked the car, and she noted there were a few people trekking up and down the boardwalk carrying cameras and binoculars. Was there a whale or a school of dolphins out there or something?

"What is it?"

"I want you to see it for yourself." He got out of the car and came around to unlatch her door. He held his hand out for her.

Seb seemed almost…giddy. And he was never giddy. He could be amused, bemused, sardonic and happy. But giddy?

She climbed out, and he opened the back door to the car and pulled out a pair of his own binoculars and a large towel.

Okay, it definitely had to be a whale or something she wouldn't normally see, which could be any number of things.

They walked down the boardwalk, and she noticed no one was in the water, which was strange. In fact, there were several people in uniforms directing the few folks that were arriving where to go.

When they got to the end of the boardwalk, one of the uniformed men asked Seb for his name, which he told them. He checked a clipboard and nodded. "Okay, go ahead, but stay behind the yellow tape and keep voices low."

It was then that she saw stakes with yellow tape snaking down the beach as far as the eye could see. What in the world?

Sebastien took her hand and led her down the line of tape, moving a long way from the boardwalk until they'd almost reached the cabana where they'd made love. That seemed so long ago.

"Did something happen?" she whispered, hoping there wasn't some kind of tragedy.

"It's in the process of happening." He stopped to look through his binoculars for a second before moving forward again. "We're almost there."

There were about fifteen people along the tape—at least as far as she could see—a much smaller number than was normal at this time of day.

Sebastien went about fifty more feet, then stopped and spread the towel out. "Let's sit here."

She had no idea what was going on, but everyone was looking at something.

Handing her the binoculars, he whispered,

"Look toward the cabana about halfway from here to there."

Putting the binoculars to her eyes, she scanned the water before realizing he hadn't said to look at the ocean. She felt him behind her, reaching forward to cover her hands with his and helping to guide her line of sight to look at…sand.

Lots and lots of sand.

"I don't—"

"Just look for a minute."

He settled himself against her hip as she stared at the white grains, straining to catch sight of whatever it was that he—and everyone else—was looking at.

Something caught her peripheral vision, near one of the flags marking a nesting site. Her gaze shifted slightly to the right as she realized something was moving. And the way it moved was familiar. It was just like…

Oh, God!

It was a baby sea turtle. The tiniest, most precious sight she'd ever seen. She followed its waddling course down the beach as it seemed to move with an unfailing confidence that defied logic.

Or did it?

Hadn't she and Seb been moving toward each other in the same way? Not knowing why or how, but only knowing it was in their nature to find the other…as surely as a sea turtle sought and found the sea.

A thought struck her, and she pulled down her binoculars to look at him. "Is that…? Is this the same…?"

"The same place we saw that sea turtle lay her eggs?" He nodded. "Yes. That is the exact nest."

Rachel's eyes filled with tears. Who knew between the time that that mama turtle had laid her eggs and the time they hatched that so much would have changed between her and Sebastien? And she loved him. So very much.

He reached forward and used his thumb to wipe a stray tear, just as something was being pressed into her other hand.

Her heart stopped, eyes widening.

Sebastien gave her a slow smile. "I wanted to wait for the perfect moment. And that moment is now."

She set the binoculars on the towel and looked down at her hand. In it was a small jeweler's box. She swallowed, her gaze swiveling from it to Seb.

He took her chin in his hand and tilted her head, placing a gentle kiss on her mouth. "I didn't have your dad's number to call and ask him. But I did talk to Claire before doing this. We talked about quite a few things."

"Her sudden trip to a friend's house?"

"Yes. That was me. I didn't know exactly when the hatch would start, so when I heard, I had to act fast."

She gulped. "A-and Claire—what did she say?"

"She said yes. To both things. As long as you did, too."

"Both things?" She had no idea what the second thing was, but cupping the tiny box in both palms, she looked at him. "Seb...are you sure? You said you wanted to take it slow."

"I realized a couple of weeks ago that this has been a long time coming. Maybe even since that first night we spent together. I don't think I could have gone any slower, do you? I love you, Rach. I always will."

Unable to speak, she looked at the box and snapped open the lid, revealing a beautiful blue gemstone surrounded by tiny diamonds. The color was the same clear hue as the ocean, and she had no doubt that Sebastien had chosen it with that in mind.

And he was right. This was the perfect time. Like those turtle eggs, which had gone from being tiny embryos to fully formed beings that were ready to start their lives, Seb and Rachel's love had gone through the same cycle. They were ready to move forward to the next stage. *She* was ready. And it was all because of Seb's love.

"So what do you say? I promised Claire I would text her as soon as I had your answer." He grinned, that one crooked tooth filling her heart with love. She didn't need a perfect smile. Or a perfect man. Because she had her own little imperfections. And despite them, Sebastien Deslaurier loved her. And she loved him.

"I say yes."

The second the words left her mouth, Seb grabbed her to him, kissing her for a long, long time. When he finally let her go, he leaned forward and whispered, "Thank you. Because my yes to Claire would have been a little harder without your yes."

She blinked, having no idea what he was talking about. "What did you say yes to?"

Seb took the ring from the box and slid it onto the fourth finger of her left hand.

"She asked me if I could be her father and to make it official. I said yes. I want to adopt her. If it's okay with you."

Her throat worked, but no sound came out. Instead, she threw her arms around him, burying her face in his neck.

He seemed to understand what she was trying to get across, because he squeezed her to him and said, "Thank you."

His words opened the door to a gift more precious than anything she could have imagined—the love of a man who would be there for her. And for Claire. Always. No matter what the cost. No matter what came their way. Like those tightly packed grounds of coffee that only revealed their true flavor when the waters of life rushed through them, her love for Seb was the same. It was strong and enduring and incredibly rich.

And it always would be.

* * * * *

*If you enjoyed this story, check out
these other great reads from
Tina Beckett*

From Wedding Guest to Bride?
One Night with the Sicilian Surgeon
Their Reunion to Remember
Starting Over with the Single Dad

All available now!